WHITEWATER

By Bill Knox

WHITEWATER

BILL KNOX

PUBLISHED FOR THE CRIME CLUB BY
DOUBLEDAY & COMPANY, INC.
GARDEN CITY, NEW YORK
1974

Knox

Library of Congress Cataloging in Publication Data
Knox, Bill, 1928–
Whitewater.
I. Title.
PZ4.K748Wf3 [PR6061.N6]   823'.9'14
ISBN 0-385-05887-X
Library of Congress Catalog Card Number 74-4899

First Edition in the United States of America

Copyright © 1974 by Bill Knox
All Rights Reserved
Printed in the United States of America

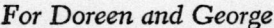

For Doreen and George

WHITE WATER

CHAPTER ONE

Gay in the summer afternoon sunlight and flapping lazily in an off-shore breeze, the flag at the fishing boat's masthead was a brilliant banner of red and gold, a message of invitation for all who could read it and understand.

But for the outsider it was a puzzle. On the bridge of Her Majesty's Fishery Protection cruiser *Marlin*, newly in from the deep water of the South Minch and now murmuring her way up the placid blue of Loch Rudha, Chief Officer Webb Carrick considered the strange banner again. It picked out that one boat from all the other bare masts in the little fishing harbour ahead, and he had a wry feeling he must be almost the only person in the fishery cruiser who didn't know its meaning. The deck party at *Marlin's* bow were already pointing and grinning. Even the thin, usually sad-eyed East Coast helmsman had begun humming under his breath, the tune a gay island lilt totally alien to the man's dour character.

The sound somehow overcame the purring note of *Marlin's* diesels. And it brought an odd, chuckling grunt from the bearded, chubbily moon-faced figure perched on the bridge command chair behind them.

"Never seen a flag like that before, mister?" demanded Captain James Shannon with a brusque amusement. He didn't wait for an answer. "Don't try looking for it in the signal book—it isn't there. But we've arrived at a good time, eh, helmsman?"

"Aye, sir." The East Coast man bared an alarmingly broken collection of teeth in an open grin but kept his eyes ahead. The channel into Port MacFarlane required care, and the unwary risked a taste of the reefs which hid just below low tide level on either quarter. "Aye, we're in luck all right."

Carrick looked from the helmsman to Shannon with a feeling of irritation, but they left it at that as if sharing a secret.

"Steer one-seven-oh," rasped Shannon suddenly. He waited till *Marlin*'s bow swung round to line up with a white cottage on a hill above the village, thumbed a silent explanation towards a broken patch of water now to starboard, a whirl of eddies and broken wavelets which marked an isolated fang of rock, then lowered himself down from the command chair. On his feet, he was surprisingly small for his build.

"You want to know about that flag, mister?" he relented.

"It would help," agreed Carrick mildly.

"That's a fisherman's wedding flag, mister." Shannon chuckled to himself with an unaccustomed humour. "From the swallow-tail length, it's a skipper who's getting hitched. Looks like you're going to sample your first island wedding, mister—and may God have mercy on the certain hangover you'll have afterwards."

Carrick grinned. The Western Isles of the Scottish coast had a tradition of hard living and harder drinking and Port MacFarlane, now near enough for him to be able to hear a dog barking somewhere ashore, was on the south-west finger of the island of Mull. On Mull, a do-it-yourself liquor still was only illicit if someone was fool enough to let it be discovered.

"How do we get invited, sir?" he asked hopefully.

"You just go—everybody goes," declared Shannon, then sought confirmation. "Correct, helmsman?"

"Aye, Captain." The helmsman nodded almost sadly. "The last wedding I went to in these parts lasted five days—or so they tell me. I only remember the first three, and I'm kind of uncertain about them."

His eyes strayed as he spoke. Shannon growled a warning, backed it with a sudden scowl, and the man stiffened again.

Two minutes later, her big twin diesels throttled back to a whisper, the fishery cruiser eased her way past Port MacFarlane's breakwater and came in to tie up at a vacant berth on the south arm of the long stone quayside. The fishing fleet lay moored and mainly deserted on the opposite side of the harbour, but there was singing and laughter and the wheeze of an accordion coming from the boat with the wedding flag. A hatch cover slid back, an arm appeared briefly, and an empty bottle went flying over the side.

"Make it watch and watch about for shore leave, mister," said Shannon thoughtfully, watching the bottle bob away. "While we're here, you can expect the whole Highland hospitality treatment. But if *Marlin* is called out I want enough of a crew aboard and sober to get her moving."

Without waiting for an answer, he strode over to the bridge wing, paused there, and saw for himself the way the fishery cruiser lay alongside the quay. A final, keen glance at the state of her mooring lines and he seemed satisfied.

"Finished with engines, sir?" queried Carrick.

"Finished." Shannon nodded and sighed a little. "If I'm needed, I'll be in my day-cabin for a spell—paperwork, mister. The usual damned Department monthly returns."

Carrick slapped the bridge telegraph level to "Stop Engines." The signal was repeated back and the diesels died with a sigh, leaving only the steady lap of water against the fishery cruiser's hull and the low background whine of her main generator.

Captain Shannon had already left the bridge. Nodding to the helmsman, who was leaning against a bulkhead and hand-rolling a cigarette, Carrick strolled past the tiny chartroom which lay aft. From there he went down the narrow companionway stair to the main deck and crossed over to the rail.

About thirty boats were moored around the harbour. They varied in size from small seine-netters to a group of big, brown-hulled drifters and many bore registration letters which showed they were far from home. But the wedding flag, flying from a new-looking medium sized drifter, had probably brought many of them from the other islands. It might even be responsible for two rusty, steel-hulled craft, isolated further back and with the appearance of pensioned-off trawlers.

Carrick lit a cigarette and relaxed, considering the drifter with the wedding flag. But a sudden loud clang of metal followed by an indignant voice raised in protest made him frown and glance aft.

Then he relaxed again with a sigh and watched the minor pantomime going on near the *Marlin*'s stern. Two deckhands were struggling to rig a water hose between the quay and the fishery cruiser, anxiously supervised by a young, fair-haired figure in an ancient, dirtied shirt and overalls. Jumbo Wills was second mate and owed his nickname to his build—and at that moment things obviously weren't going his way.

"Don't make a production out of it," pleaded Wills to his helpers. "All it needs is some coaxing."

One of the deckhands muttered under his breath. Wills flushed, waved the men aside, and battled with the hose connection on his own for a few moments. Then he stood back and gestured triumphantly.

"Connected—just like that! See what I mean?" Swinging round, he signalled to another seaman waiting on the quayside. "All right, let's have that water!"

The flattened hose-length filled out and quivered as the quayside hydrant opened to full pressure. Wills beamed. Then, suddenly, the hose nozzle broke loose under that pressure. In an instant the hose-length was jerking and twisting like a giant snake and a powerful jet of water was spurting across the decks one moment then towards the sky the next.

Jumbo Wills and his men disappeared behind a curtain of water while he howled for the hydrant to be shut off again. Almost reluctantly, the man on the quayside obeyed and the hose collapsed with a quiver on the flooded deck. A final trickle of water still came from the nozzle while the second mate stared in dazed disbelief.

"Mr. Wills, you're supposed to wash in your own time," hailed Carrick. "And you forgot the soap."

A small audience who had gathered on the quayside began laughing. Brick-red, soaked to the skin, Wills scowled at the two dripping deckhands who looked back at him with a bland innocence.

The trio got to work again on the hose connection and Carrick, still chuckling, switched his attention back to the harbour and what lay beyond it.

Port MacFarlane was a thin straggle of white-walled, slate-roofed houses and cottages, most of them scattered along the shore. A few larger buildings were grouped near the harbour and one or two isolated farmhouses clung to the lower slopes of the heather-covered hills above. In two short years of Fishery Protection service Webb Carrick reckoned he must have seen at least a hundred identical fishing villages along the Scottish north-west coast. There were probably that number again still waiting him among the islands.

But even without the promise of the wedding flag, he reckoned *Marlin*'s crew had been glad to see harbour this time. For ten days the slim grey fishery cruiser and her crew of twenty-four had been on routine patrol along the Hebridean chain of islands. Most of that time the weather had teetered on the edge of gale-force, constant lumping green seas breaking hard against *Marlin*'s plating then draining from her scuppers in torrents with each following heave.

That meant every man aboard had had his full share of being bruised and battered and soaked times without number. Without anything in particular to show for it except a couple of Polish trawlers boarded for illegal fishing south of Barra Head. Their skippers had slipped their fishing warps and abandoned their nets, there was no evidence left, and they'd parted in mutual ill-humour.

An ordinary, dull, routine patrol—Carrick grimaced at the thought and rested his elbows against the rail.

Some ash from the cigarette fell on his naval uniform jacket and he brushed it away. Under the jacket he wore a once white wool sweater and a salt-stained cap with the gold anchor badge of Fishery Protection was shoved back from his forehead while his feet, in short-length seaboots, were unconsciously placed apart to meet a deck-sway which no longer existed. For the rest, Webb Carrick was stockily built and five feet ten in height with the inevitable weather-bronzed face of his trade.

It was a broad-boned face, with dark brown eyes and darker brown hair. A face with a usually easy-going expression yet with

5

lips a little too thin to allow any idea he could be pushed around—
even Captain Shannon had discovered that fact, and had come
to terms with it. But at the same time, two years in Fishery Protection had brought more lines of experience round Carrick's eyes
at the age of thirty-one than all the Merchant Navy deep-sea
time he'd put in beforehand.

Still against the rail, he drew on the cigarette again and was
flicking the remaining stub away when a pointedly heavy throat-
clearing noise came from behind him. Glancing round, he
nodded a welcome to the bulky giant who accepted it as an invitation to join him at the rail.

"I was wonderin' about shore leave, sir." Petty Officer William
"Clapper" Bell, six feet plus of Glasgow-Irish innocence and
Marlin's bo'sun, tried hard to remove any trace of personal interest from his rumbling voice and rugged features. "Mind you, it
doesn't much matter to me. I couldn't raise the price of a beer, if
you know what I mean—"

"Again?" asked Carrick wearily. "Which was it this time, Clapper? Poker with the port watch or the engine room's Saturday
night dice game?"

"No, I kept clear of them. But cookie cleaned me out at three-
card brag." Clapper Bell grimaced and scratched his close-cropped
ginger hair at the injustice of life. "Still, the crew are askin' if
they—"

"Tell them shore leave is watch and watch about," said Carrick,
cutting him short. "But warn them that the Old Man says we're
remaining on standby—warn them and make sure they remember
it."

"I'll do that," Clapper Bell nodded then paused hopefully.
"Mind you, if I was ashore wi' some money in my pocket I could
make sure of keeping an eye on things. But, like I said—"

Carrick sighed and reached into his hip pocket. Clapper Bell
was his other half in *Marlin's* scuba diving team, and that kind of
partnership bred its own style of discipline.

"Two quid do for starters?" he asked.

"As always." A massive paw swallowed the notes as he brought them out and the bo'sun grinned happily. "See the tangle Jumbo Wills got into wi' that hose, sir?"

"He'll maybe discover somewhere new to put it next time," answered Carrick, deadpan.

"And do himself a horrible injury?" Bell chuckled at the thought then thumbed across the harbour towards the fluttering red and gold of the wedding flag. "Has Captain Shannon told you yet?"

"Told me what?" Carrick sensed the bo'sun was enjoying himself.

"He's a crafty old basket," said Clapper Bell softly, with a quick glance around to make sure no-one was near. "We come in here just by chance, on routine patrol, right? And we're maybe going to lie over for a couple o' days, right?"

Carrick nodded. "So?"

"This wedding is tomorrow. The girl's daddy is a long-time sea-going pal of the Old Man's—and the whole damned village knew we were due to arrive this afternoon." Bell sucked his lips in open admiration. "He's crafty all right."

Carrick shaped a silent whistle. "You're sure?"

"Would I say anything if I wasn't?" The bo'sun was hurt at the thought. "I saw this fellow on the quayside as we were berthing—"

From Clapper Bell, that made it official. The Glasgow-Irishman's personal grapevine seemed to stretch from the islands to the Admiralty, always with uncanny accuracy.

"What else did you hear?" asked Carrick, considering Captain Shannon's flawless timing with a new respect.

"The girl's name is Mhari MacLean. She's back home after working in London for a spell an' she's marrying a skipper called Roddy Fraser." Bell shook his head, frowning slightly. "I don't know much about him. There was a Black Dan Fraser workin' an old boat out of Mallig for a few years and he was a wild basket. But whether there's any connection—"

"You'll find out," agreed Carrick and eased himself off the rail. "I'm going below. Just remember that's another two quid you owe me."

"It's as safe as in the bank," assured the bo'sun fervently. He

7

watched Carrick go, then ambled back towards the watering party. With luck, and a little gratitude on Jumbo Wills' part, his finances might show a further improvement.

. . . . .

Harbour rounds was a routine Captain Shannon insisted on whenever *Marlin* reached port, a job that fell on Webb Carrick's shoulders. It meant spending about an hour touring every department of the fishery cruiser, part inspecting, part listening to moans, making sure that she was equally ready to receive visitors or head out to sea.

The pounding she had taken from the Minch had left a few scars and breakages, but most of these were already being made good. He found a few more, put men to work clearing them, then was finished.

The steward had the usual pot of coffee bubbling on a stove in *Marlin*'s tiny wardroom. He helped himself to a cup, drank it, then took a second cup along to his own small 'tween decks cabin aft. The door to the next cabin was closed, which meant that Pettigrew, the junior second mate though a man in middle age, was catching up on some sleep.

That, he decided, was Pettigrew's main occupation in life. Kicking his own cabin door shut in momentary irritation, Carrick wearily eased out of his seaboots, and lay back on the bunk for a few minutes' rest.

The second cup of coffee was cold when Carrick rose again. He slipped into shoes, put a new pack of cigarettes in one pocket, glanced round the little, sparsely furnished cabin with the shelf of books above the bunk and the wet-weather oilskins hung beside the door, and decided to go ashore.

He was back on the main deck and heading towards the gangway, where a leading hand was posted, when Jumbo Wills suddenly barred his way.

"Webb, about this wedding tomorrow," began Wills. "Clapper says—"

Carrick stopped him. "He already told me."

"But what happens if we're called out halfway through the

celebrations?" Wills' young, freckled face contorted in a frown. "Who takes *Marlin* out of here?"

"That's a point," agreed Carrick. "Let's say you do, Jumbo—single-handed if necessary. It could be your big chance for fame."

"I could do without it." Wills rubbed a dirty hand down the front of his equally dirty shirt and sighed. "With my kind of luck I don't need to go looking for trouble."

Carrick made a commiserating noise and left him.

On shore, he looked around with interest. You could learn a lot about most fishing villages from their quaysides and Port Mac-Farlane was no exception. There was an indefinable feel of prosperity about the place. Here and there he saw nets spread to dry or repair, but they were in a minority beside the mounds of well-kept lobster creels. There were high stacks of the ventilated wooden boxes in which lobsters, carefully packed in ice, were shipped off live to market.

A big white herring gull flapped down, landed almost at his feet, stared at him for a moment with insolent, beady eyes, then flew off again to join the scores of others wheeling raucously overhead. Carrick walked on, the familiar smells of kerosene and diesel fuel, of rotting seaweed and fish offal reaching his nostrils while he noted the fresh paint on the quayside sheds and number of new cars parked around.

Then, instinctively, his eyes strayed back to *Marlin*'s high, raked bow and squat single funnel.

Even after two years, he still marvelled at the size of her task. One hundred and eighty feet long, she covered an average of 17,000 sea miles a year up and down the long, straggling West coast of Scotland, with its island chains and reefs, its whirlpools and fierce tidal overraces. The West coast was generally rated among the most treacherous in the world. Just as in fishing terms it was one of the richest, the scene of a multi-million pound industry in which every skipper was a hard-headed individualist. An individualist who saw Fishery Protection's regulations as just another damned nuisance almost as low as the Inland Revenue or the perfidious wholesale buyers.

Yet *Marlin* and her kind represented the rule of law almost single-handed along that dangerous sweep of waters. She had no guns on her decks, only the mounting plates ready for war emergency use. But she had authority enough in the thirty knots speed of her twin 2,000 h.p. diesels, the Blue Ensign with the gold Fisheries badge which flew at her square-cut stern and, above all, the sheer personality of her captain.

Shannon rated as a Superintendent of Fisheries, with the power to be his own judge and jury in most fishing disputes. He had four hundred tons of ship, a life-time's skill and experience, and a crew of twenty plus three watch-keeping officers. They were his tools to keep order along a coastline where the only things sharper than the reefs were the wits of the fishermen who dared them for their catches.

Unpredictable fishermen, island style—spoiling for a fight one day, ready to swop a basket of fresh-caught fish for coffee or cigarettes the next.

Out on the harbour water, a milk-blue jellyfish was drifting in towards a stranded death on the shingle. Carrick watched it, his mind going back to his own introduction to Fishery Protection.

He'd been out of a job, a newly won master's ticket in his pocket but no ship in sight, when he'd been called to a Department interview in Edinburgh. He'd left that interview with a new black warrant card as an Assistant Superintendent of Fisheries.

"A sea-going policeman with Civil Service pension rights if you last long enough," was how Shannon had summarised the job when he'd reported aboard *Marlin*. "We don't know what you're like, but when you're out among the islands, whitewater style, we'll find out soon enough."

"Whitewater style" had been an initially terrifying new aspect of sheer seamanship, which could make commonplace a full-tilt night chase after an offending boat in conditions no sane crew would have tackled in daylight. Or keeping to a patrol schedule in a full gale, because the fishing boats would stay out too.

And all the rest. Learning a whole catalogue of rules and regulations which governed net sizes and permitted gear, seasonal bans, restrictions and limits, poaching by foreign craft—and the regular addition of tragedy or disaster or the need to avert potentially bloody conflict between rival factions. Always with the knowledge that no self-respecting fisherman gave a damn about bending or stretching the rules if they stood between him and the chance of a rich catch.

Unless, of course, *Marlin* or one of her sisters was near enough to make him hesitate.

Smiling at the thought, Carrick walked on until the drifter with the wedding flag was only a few yards along the quayside. Accordion music was still coming from her fo'c'sle cabin, backed by voices and laughter. The broad-beamed little vessel's name was *Razorbill* and some amateur artist had painted a stylised version of her seabird namesake along both sides of the wheelhouse, catching the distinctive whetted back of the bird and the characteristic splash of white below the black, eager head.

And the drifter had to have a crew proudly devoted to her care—from immaculately coiled ropes to scrubbed deck and fresh paintwork, she looked more like an exhibition model than a boat which had to earn a living. Unless you counted the tell-tale marks of use and wear around her derrick boom and hatch-covers and the way in which her wooden hull already bore scars which even a paint-brush couldn't quite hide.

"Hey, you up there!" The hail came from the *Razorbill*'s fore-deck and he saw a figure grinning up at him. "Come on down, friend—everybody's welcome!"

"To what?" queried Carrick easily, going nearer.

"To a good dram that'll help ease another poor idiot on his way to wedded bliss." The man below was tall and thin, with long, black, shoulder-length hair, a white-toothed grin, and a deep baritone voice which held a wisp of West Highland lilt. "May the Lord have mercy on him—the witch he's marrying will have the clampers on him good and proper."

"Then it's a good cause," agreed Carrick cheerfully.

There was an iron ladder set in the quayside and he climbed down, reaching the drifter's deck in a final swinging jump. The thin, tall figure stood waiting, thumbs hitched in the broad leather belt round his middle. Face bronzed the colour of well-tanned leather, the stranger wore an old red wool shirt with black jeans and ancient basketball boots.

"You're off the 'queer fellow,' right?" he said.

"Carrick, chief officer," nodded Carrick, accepting the islander tag for a protection cruiser. "And you?"

"Dan Fraser—today's host and tomorrow's best man. It's my wee brother Roddy that gets hitched in the morning. Come and meet him, Carrick—" Fraser half-turned to lead the way then stopped, eyes twinkling "—we had your bo'sun aboard half an hour back. God, that man can drink!"

"He works at it," agreed Carrick.

"Like it goes with the job." The fisherman beckoned and Carrick followed him along the deck then down a narrow hatchway into the fo'c'sle cabin.

Lined with bunks on each side and with a long table in the middle, the cabin was generous in size in terms of ordinary crew space. But at that moment it seemed close to bulging, the air blue with tobacco smoke and reeking of liquor, at least a score of men drinking or singing or trying to make themselves heard in the general din. The accordionist, a fat, bald fisherman, was standing on a chair and making up in noise for anything he lacked in skill.

"A drink first—" Fraser propelled Carrick towards the table, which held an assortment of stoneware flagons and scattered bottles "—hey, a drink for the Fishery snoop, Archie."

Whoever Archie was, a tin mug had a liberal measure of what looked like whisky poured into it from a flagon and was shoved into Carrick's hand. As Dan Fraser propelled him through the ruck again, Carrick spotted a couple of *Marlin's* stokers busy back-slapping a fisherman and laughing.

"Here we are, Carrick," declared Dan Fraser happily. "Meet my wee brother, Roddy. Roddy, stand up, damn you—there's another Fishery snoop come to drink your health!"

A younger version of Fraser but if anything even taller struggled up from the bunk where he'd been sitting. His face had a slightly glazed look but he grinned a welcome, the mug in his hand coming up.

"*Slainche*, mister," he said with a slight slur in his voice.

"Wedded bliss," agreed Carrick and took a gulp from his own mug. Next moment he had the distinct impression the top of his skull had been forcibly removed and that sheer liquid fire was etching a way down his throat. He swallowed hard, eyes watering, and stared at the brothers. "What is this stuff?"

"Best triple-run malt from the mountains, courtesy of a cousin of ours," said Dan Fraser proudly. "You won't often taste its like."

"I'll believe that part." Carrick tried another cautious mouthful.

"Well, maybe the stuff is a shade young yet," admitted Dan Fraser with a mild reluctance. "A month or two maturing would have made a difference, but there wasn't time for that kind of ageing."

"Not for when we needed it." Roddy Fraser grinned around the cabin, swaying slightly. "Still, nobody's complaining. Do drink up, Carrick. There's plenty more."

"How about saving some for after the wedding?" asked Carrick, raising his voice above the din.

"No need, man," said the young bridegroom happily. "Mhari's father takes care of every bottle then—all bought wholesale an' legal and shipped from Glasgow. Though mind you, he's done nothing but moan since he got the bill for the stuff." He stopped, hiccuped, then clutched at Carrick for support as he almost over-balanced.

"Easy now, Roddy." Dan Fraser guided his brother into an upright position again then turned to Carrick, eyes twinkling. "Like I said, the poor idiot deserves a good send-off."

The accordion struck up another ragged tune in the background and out of the jam of bodies a fisherman pushed through to join them. Slack-mouthed and bleary-eyed, he peered at Carrick through the haze of smoke.

"I know you," he said owlishly. "You're the bamfpot who—aye, you're the bamfpot who boarded the *Anna B.* last month."

He recognised the man. His name was Christie and when *Marlin*'s boarding party had reached the *Anna B.*, a battered seine-netter with a reputed sideline in smuggling, Christie had gone for them with an iron bar.

13

"No hard feelings, bamfpot." Christie grinned, hiccuped, and stayed where he was. "Ever caught the Frasers at their tricks?"

"Not so far." Carrick shook his head. "We can't be everywhere."

"Wouldn't matter if you were." Dan Fraser laughed, unperturbed. "We're two independent, law-abiding gentlemen of business. Particularly now, eh, Roddy?"

"Yes." The younger man sat on the bunk again and made an attempt at an intelligent scowl. "We've a new boat and money in the bank—all done by thinking, Carrick. Thinking an'—an' marketing."

"Thanks to Roddy's brains and my brawn," confirmed his brother cheerfully. "Firstly, we packed in the net-fishing and decided lobsters were our game. That's where the real money is around here. Then we worked out the best way to market them— best for us, at any rate."

"I saw plenty of lobster creels along the quay," nodded Carrick.

"But few of them ours," declared Roddy Fraser eagerly, his voice still slurring. "The other boats can do what they want but we say creel-traps are old-fashioned. We know where to look an' we go right down an' catch them on the bottom."

"Scuba style?" Carrick showed his surprise. Aqualung diving for lobsters wasn't new, but it usually caused trouble in the shape of angry creel fishers.

"Scuba, storage, and then air freight," confirmed Dan Fraser briskly. "Get Roddy to tell you about it—" he paused and grinned "—but when he's sober."

"If he does, be sure an' tell the rest of us afterwards," slurred the fisherman named Christie, swaying between them again and wagging a finger. "Plenty aroun' here would listen."

Another fisherman grabbed his arm and muttered, but Christie shook him off.

"Look at them," he invited the fo'c'sle in general. "The lucky, lucky Frasers. Except whose lobsters do they—" he stopped, looked at his finger in puzzlement, then seemed to remember the rest "— aye, whose lobsters do they get?"

Dan Fraser's smile died and he stroked a slow hand over his long black hair.

"Knock it off, Christie," he said softly.

"The hell I will!" Christie was pugnaciously unrepentant. "Plenty of us know how it's done down there. You get the flamin' lobsters—an' the other boats get the empty creels. Creels that you've already dived down to empty an'—"

Dan Fraser hardly seemed to move. But his right fist took Christie hard on the jaw and sent him tumbling to the deck.

The accordion died with a squeal and the fo'c's'le went silent.

"You pair o' chanty wrastlin', thievin' scum!" Face contorted, Christie struggled up again. One hand scooped under his work jacket and came out clutching a hook-bladed gutting knife. "This time, I'll teach you!"

He took a lurching step nearer, the knife slicing a wavering arc through the smoke-filled air. Then, as he moved again, Carrick threw the mug of whisky in his hand straight into the man's face.

Momentarily blinded, eyes stinging, Christie bellowed in surprise. He tried to wipe his face with his sleeve—and at the same moment the fisherman who had warned him earlier smashed a beer bottle over his head. Beer and broken glass spattered the nearest onlookers while Christie slumped down, thudding on the deck where he lay still.

"Och, I didn't belt him too hard, Dan," said the man who had wielded the bottle. "No sense in spoilin' a good party, eh?"

The accordion was playing again as Carrick helped Dan Fraser drag Christie's sack-like weight out onto the open deck.

"Here will do." Fraser dropped Christie face down on a tarpaulin cover, considered the limp form angrily, then turned to Carrick with a shrug of disgust.

"You get one like him at every party. But about what he said—"

"There's always somebody who doesn't like the other fellow winning?" suggested Carrick mildly.

"Something like that. Maybe I pushed things a bit by thumping him, but that's how it goes." Dan Fraser used a foot to prod the unconscious man, who still showed no signs of stirring. "He'll be all right. Christie's skull is solid bone all the way through."

"It sounded that way," agreed Carrick almost absently, his attention switching to the quayside above. A girl was standing there,

15

looking down on the scene with a cool amusement. Nudging Fraser, he glanced in his direction. "You've a visitor."

"Eh?" Fraser looked up, swore softly under his breath, then forced a slightly apprehensive grin and waved a greeting. "Hello, Tara. Like to join the party?"

"Not if that's a sample lying down there," she said dryly. Tall and slim and in her mid-twenties, she had short, fair hair which had been ruffled by the breeze. Wearing a leather jacket over red trousers and a white, ribbed wool sweater, she had an oval, slightly freckled face and a wide mouth which was trying hard to stay disapproving. "What happened to him?"

"Just a wee shade too much to drink, that's all. But we're having a fine, friendly party." Fraser decided to enlist support, and quickly. "Tara, this is Chief Officer Carrick from the fishery cruiser. Ask him if you don't believe me."

"It's as peaceful as a Sunday School outing," said Carrick blandly.

"See?" said Fraser triumphantly. "Carrick, the lady thinking the worst is Tara Grant, tomorrow's bridesmaid."

"If we've still got a bridegroom," she countered dryly. "Dan, I've a message from the radiant bride. What the hell has her alcoholic husband-to-be done with that suitcase he said he'd deliver this morning?"

Dan Fraser winced. "I forgot, Tara. Roddy asked me to get it over to her house, but—"

"But you tripped over a bottle?" She sighed resignedly. "Where is the thing? I'll take it with me—my car's at the harbour parking lot."

"Hold on." Fraser strode quickly towards the wheelhouse, yanked open the door, then reached inside and dragged out a bulky canvas travel bag. He came back holding the bag aloft. "Roddy packed it last night."

"His going-away outfit," said Tara Grant dryly. "If I were Mhari I'd settle for an anchor to tie round his middle—then drop him overboard somewhere deep."

"But the lucky man's not marrying you," countered Dan Fraser

16

with a bellow of laughter. "Stand back a bit and I'll heave this up." He felt the weight again, then hesitated. "Think you can manage it on your own? I—uh—I'd bring it for you, but with all these lads below—" he stopped, a fresh burst of accordion music and a chorus which was a particularly bawdy version of the *Road to the Isles* underlining what he meant.

"The bridesmaid wore pink taffeta and a plaster cast." Tara Grant sighed. "Go ahead—I'm expendable."

Carrick chuckled at the look on her face. "I'll take it. I'm due back on *Marlin* anyway."

"I'd appreciate the favour." Fraser handed him the bag without argument. It was heavier than Carrick had expected and the fisherman quickly explained, "There's a thing or two in there that Roddy's been given as wedding presents—Mhari hasn't seen them yet."

Carrick nodded, shifted the carrying loops of the bag to the crook of his arm, and climbed up the iron-runged ladder to the quayside.

"Come back later, man," called Fraser, waving a hand in farewell and turning away towards the fo'c'sle hatch. "We'll save a jar or two for you—that's a promise."

"It sounds more like a threat," said Tara Grant. She combed a wisp of fair hair back from her forehead with one hand and smiled. "Thanks. Do I call you 'sir' or Chief Officer or what?"

"Webb will do." Carrick considered her with unconcealed appreciation. Tara Grant's eyes were grey, her skin golden, and she filled the ribbed sweater as if the knitter had had her in mind with every stitch. A neat waist, slim but far from boyish hips and a relaxed confidence as she moved added up to a distinct feeling that *Marlin's* visit to Port MacFarlane had taken on a new dimension. "Where's your car?"

"Not far away." She started off, Carrick at her side, then slowed again and gave a murmur of interest.

A small white speedboat was bouncing its way over the waves into harbour with two men in bright orange life-jackets standing in its cockpit. As the speedboat came inside the breakwater its

17

engine was throttled back. Wake fading to a ripple, it manoeuvred in towards the opposite quay and edged against the stonework just astern of *Marlin*.

One of the figures scrambled along the hull to attach a mooring line to a quayside ring. The other, taller and wearing a yachting cap, saw Tara Grant and gave a wave in her direction. She returned it cheerfully.

"That's Frank Farrell," she explained for Carrick's benefit. "Maybe you've heard of him."

"No." He considered her mildly. "Any special reason why I should?"

"Maybe not," she admitted, watching the boat. "Frank is in the property game—down south mainly, but right now he's prospecting up here. Small Highland estates or little islands—particularly islands. His theory is your genuine city tycoons are getting round to see them as the newest thing in status symbols."

Carrick nodded. The trend was already under way and there was plenty of room for it provided the buyers had money. He thought how the vast Hebridean chain showed on the charts, hundreds of islands from rocky, spray-swept outcrops to pleasant green havens which could cover several square miles. Isolation and emigration had left all but the largest uninhabited, incapable of providing a living.

"And how about the boat?" he asked.

"It belongs to Dirk Peters—the man with him," she explained. "Dirk has a tumbledown family mansion and some hill land north of here, but he's based in England. He runs a yacht marina on the south coast. They're both in Port MacFarlane for the wedding."

"Friends of the bride?" asked Carrick innocently. The speed-boat moored, both men were climbing ashore.

"Something like that. We made up a foursome with them in London for a spell." Tara Grant smiled at the memory. "Mhari was fresh down from the islands and we were working in television together, on the secretarial side. She'd met Dirk a few times on Mull, and he turned up with Frank."

"Cosy," murmured Carrick.

"We shared a few dates," she shrugged. "But then Mhari came

back to Mull for a holiday about three months ago. Roddy Fraser was the legendary childhood sweetheart who just happened to be around again, and that was that."

"The original happy ending?"

She nodded quizzically. "Any more questions?"

"Not right now," he mused. "Maybe later."

"I had that feeling." Tara Grant considered him for a moment, a faint twinkle in her grey eyes. "Now you know, can we move on? Mhari's likely to think I've stayed boozing with the Fraser clan."

He followed her the rest of the way to a small yellow Triumph sports car. It had the hood down, and he eased the bag into the luggage space behind the twin bucket seats.

"Thanks." She slipped in behind the driving wheel, started the engine, then let it tick over. "Your captain will be at the wedding— how about you? They don't worry too much about formal invitations around here."

"I've heard," he agreed solemnly.

"Then try and make it." She slid the Triumph into gear, kept the clutch pedal down for a moment, and revved the engine. "From some of the stories about what can happen afterwards, I could use a bodyguard."

"You've got your friend Farrell," reminded Carrick. "Or do I mean Peters?"

"Frank Farrell was mine. Was—past tense." She grimaced up at him. "Everyone makes mistakes."

The engine revved again and the car moved off, scattering gravel. Carrick watched it turn left into the main street, then, as it disappeared, he walked back towards *Marlin*.

On the way, he encountered the men from the speedboat. They gave him a brief glance of minimal curiosity as they passed and he drew a faint nod from Frank Farrell, who was thin-faced, good-looking in a tall, lanky way, and had long, fair sideburns which stopped just short of his chin. Dirk Peters, smaller and thick-set with a pugilistic nose, walked with a bouncing, hurried, step to keep up with his long-legged companion.

Carrick glanced back as he reached *Marlin*'s gangway and saw both men were heading towards the *Razorbill*. He wondered briefly how their city palates would react to the Frasers' raw liquor and was still smiling at the thought as he went aboard.

"Chief—" the seaman on gangway watch met him as he stepped on deck "—the Old Man is looking for you."

Carrick raised an eyebrow. "Trouble?"

The man shrugged slightly in a way that meant he wasn't paid to find out. "He had a visitor, one of them locals. That's all I know, sir."

"Tell him I'm back," ordered Carrick. "I'll be along in a couple of minutes."

Puzzled, he made a detour to the bridge and looked in at the chartroom. No fresh signals were entered in the radio log, the weather report they'd received at 1600 hours still stood and the usual readiness status check-list left by Jumbo Wills showed *Marlin* free of problems. He sighed. Whatever was on Shannon's mind, at least he knew a few of the answers to possible questions.

·   ·   ·   ·   ·

Captain James Shannon's day-cabin was immediately below the bridge. It was moderately large, plainly furnished, and totally practical from its spotless white paintwork to the gleaming brass of the roll pendulum and repeater compass hanging above his leather topped desk. The only intrusion was a large tomato plant which bushed upward from a wooden pot to obscure one porthole. Shannon's wife had brought the tomato plant aboard after *Marlin*'s last refit and Shannon loathed it, feeding the thing on a deliberate mixture of tobacco ash and cold coffee. But the tomato plant thrived—and he seemed reluctant to risk domestic bliss by trying more drastic action.

When Carrick knocked and entered, Shannon was standing at a table in the middle of the cabin. A large, opened parcel was spread out on the table and the small, bearded figure was scowling down at its contents.

"Close the door, mister," said Shannon gruffly, without looking up. "Come and take a look at this."

Carrick obeyed. Inside the parcel was a large crystal vase,

plainly expensive but probably the most ugly crystal vase ever made.

"Like it?" demanded Shannon.

"It's unusual," said Carrick cautiously.

"It's bloody awful," snarled Shannon, disgusted. "I know that—but my wife picked it." He closed the wrappings with a frown then cleared his throat. "This wedding tomorrow, mister. I—uh—knew about it before we got here. Knew about it, nothing more. But—uh—it seemed a good idea to be prepared."

"In case we should call in," nodded Carrick innocently. "You wouldn't want to put something like that vase in the mail, sir."

"True." Shannon coloured a little. "The—ah—the girl's father, Jimsy MacLean, is an old friend of mine, mister. He was captain on a tramp steamer on the South Atlantic run for God knows how many years, then he got lucky—towed in a damned great oil tanker that looked like sinking, and got enough in salvage money to retire. Like to meet him?"

"At the wedding?"

"That's going to be a shambles." Shannon dismissed the idea out of hand. "No, tonight. Jimsy MacLean was aboard half an hour ago, and invited me to his house for dinner. They're having a few friends, and I said I'd bring you along for moral support."

Carrick smothered a grin. "I'd like that."

"Good." Shannon took a deep breath of relief. "Then you can carry this damned box when we go—be ready for twenty hundred hours and make sure Pettigrew is awake by then. He's officer of the watch."

"I will, sir." Carrick nodded and turned towards the door.

"I'm not finished, mister." Shannon's growl brought him back. "I heard you went over to the *Razorbill*."

"I had a drink with the Frasers, yes." Carrick waited.

For a moment Shannon stood silent, hands clasped behind his back, his lips sucking a stray tendril of beard. Then the round moon-face seemed to come to a decision.

"How were things over there?"

"Lively, sir," said Carrick, sensing more behind the question.

"Any—uh—atmosphere. Unusual feel about it, I mean?"

"A drunk got laid out. He thought the Frasers were catching too many lobsters to be true," said Carrick briefly.

"That's all?" Shannon was disappointed. He sucked the same tendril of beard for another moment. "I met Black Dan Fraser once—boarded him for suspected seal-poaching, but he was clean. The brother Roddy, tomorrow's bridegroom, I've only heard about."

"They seem to make quite a partnership," mused Carrick.

Shannon nodded. "With Roddy, the younger one, acting as skipper on the *Razorbill*. Didn't you think that unusual?"

Carrick shrugged. "Dan Fraser said Roddy was the brains aboard."

"True, from what Captain MacLean told me." Shannon smiled grimly. "The old story, mister. Father killed in the war, older brother stays home to earn a living, younger brother gets an education—then comes back and takes over. Their mother died a couple of years back." He seemed lost in thought again, then gave Carrick a sudden, piercing glance. "Mister, I've a reason for wanting you along tonight."

"Sir?"

"Jimsy MacLean is an old friend, like I said." Shannon pursed his lips. "He sat in this cabin, looking worried sick about something yet trying to tell me everything was sweetness and light."

"Father-of-the-bride nerves?"

Shannon dismissed the notion with contempt. "Mister, Jimsy MacLean is one of the old school, when they built men out of solid oak and whipcord, not plastic and hair-ribbons. And he happens to be wandering around with a bulge in his hip pocket that isn't any whisky flask. I want to know why the hell he needs to pack what looked like a revolver."

"Shotguns are more in style for weddings," mused Carrick.

Shannon wasn't amused. "I've a hunch there's something wrong, mister, and I want to know what it is before we sail. Understand?"

Carrick sighed and nodded. "I could put Clapper Bell to work trying to find out, sir."

"I already did," said Shannon shortly. "Twenty hundred hours, mister. And you'll keep your eyes open—that's all."

Carrick left him. The wind had dropped when he went out on deck and the wedding flag on the *Razorbill* was hanging sad and limp. He looked at it and shook his head wryly.

Captain James Shannon had his faults. But his hunches had an uncanny habit of being right.

CHAPTER TWO

Early evening in the Hebridean summer is a time when the sun, still tracking its way down towards the horizon, turns the sea into a glitter of rippling golden damask. The air carries the scent of heather from the hills as the land begins to cool and the big gulls make a last crying, circling foray over the water in search of food before settling for the night. Night, which in turn is the time of the smaller birds who feed along the shore-line.

Aboard *Marlin*, the air carried something else—the pungent smell of badly burned stew, the main component of the evening meal for the starboard watch. The fishery cruiser's cook had stubbornly claimed his share of shore leave and his sole assistant, a young galley hand, had a notorious ability for spoiling anything which involved more than boiling water.

Webb Carrick sniffed the sad result as he left his cabin moments before the scheduled twenty hundred hours. He was newly shaved, he wore a clean shirt, and he'd matched it with his best uniform jacket. The burning smell wafting along the 'tween decks companionway was a good enough reason on its own to feel glad he was eating ashore. But there was also, more important, a fairly certain chance of seeing Tara Grant again—and he'd take the other purpose Captain Shannon had in mind as things shaped.

Spruce and already impatient, Shannon was waiting by the gangway when he emerged on deck. So was Pettigrew, the thin, sad-faced junior second mate, and a couple of seamen were working with paint-brushes nearer the bow where *Marlin*'s grey paintwork still showed signs of what had happened on the Minch patrol.

"Right, mister, take this and for God's sake don't drop it," was

Shannon's greeting. He shoved the cardboard box containing the crystal vase into Carrick's hands then turned to Pettigrew. "Everything clear?"

"Yes, sir." Pettigrew nodded wearily. Untidy and permanently tired, with an edge of wispy grey hair showing beneath his hat, he was a minor mystery aboard the fishery cruiser. At the age of fifty he'd packed in a desk job and come back to sea as *Marlin's* junior officer for some reason of his own. "We stay on normal readiness but I take no independent action."

"And you get word to me immediately if anything happens," emphasised Shannon grimly. "We should be back by midnight, but if not the same orders apply to Mr. Wills when he relieves you. Understood?"

"Yes, sir." Pettigrew's nostrils twitched as the burning smell from the galley reached him. He gave a noise like a sigh. "Enjoy yourself."

Shannon led the way down the gangway, stopped for a moment on the quayside to frown back at his command with a touch of misgiving, then set off at a brisk pace.

The harbour was quiet, the ranks of fishing boats swaying gently in the slight swell while their mooring lines creaked, and the plump, bearded little figure hummed under his breath as they walked along. But as they left the harbour area and reached the start of the village Shannon slowed a little.

"There's a couple more things I'd better mention, mister," he said with a gruff embarrassment. "Captain MacLean and I started as baby-faced cadets aboard the same rust-bucket tramp steamer. So he's an old friend. But years can change a man, and he's a stubborn, opinionated devil when it comes up his back."

Carrick nodded, though the same description could have been applied to Shannon.

"The other thing is that—ah—" Shannon hesitated and cleared his throat "—well, Jimsy MacLean may spin some wild stories about the things we did in those old days. The kind of stories best forgotten, mister. He's liable to exaggerate."

"That happens, sir." Carrick stayed wooden-faced with an effort.

"Good." Shannon relaxed a little. "Still, he also happens to be a damned good seaman. When he brought in that oil tanker, it was with a ship less than half its size and against a gale that would have terrified most skippers."

"How much did he clear in salvage money?" asked Carrick, shifting his grip on the precious cardboard box as they went on down the little main street.

"Enough." Shannon's voice was unusually wry. "The tanker owners were Greeks, the kind who count their pennies, but he had them over a barrel. His share was close on a hundred thousand pounds, and that's enough to let any man retire in comfort."

Webb Carrick found it easy enough to guess what was going through Shannon's mind. In less than a couple of years it would be Shannon's turn to "swallow the anchor" and Department pensions weren't exactly scaled to provide gracious living. In his case, retirement would probably mean a small cottage somewhere with his wife and her tomato plants, though it was hard to imagine anyone like Shannon damped down to just one more old man pottering around filling in time between meals.

But it would happen. Department regulations were cast-iron, regardless of individuals.

Port MacFarlane might have been asleep as they walked through it. Only the two village bars were noisy, and most of the custom was from the boats in harbour plus a sprinkling of *Marlin*'s crew. The villagers were saving their energy for the next day's wedding festivities.

At the far end of the street the narrow road began to climb steeply, away from the hill. As they went on, a girl emerged from one of the last cottages. She was young and tanned and dressed in a light cotton dress, and she smiled as she saw them. A boy her own age appeared from the same doorway. His glance was less friendly as he started up a motor cycle. The girl scrambled on the pillion behind him and the machine roared off in a way which had her grabbing for the rider's waist while her skirt whipped high against her thighs.

Carrick chuckled, remembering an unprintable old verse about

27

slow girls and fast bikes. But part of his mind was still occupied in another direction.

"How does Captain MacLean feel about getting Roddy Fraser as a son-in-law, sir?" he asked.

"Happy enough, just stunned by the cost," shrugged Shannon. "But he'll miss the girl afterwards. Mhari is an only child and her mother died a few years back." He frowned as if calculating. "She'll be about twenty-three now, dark and good-looking like her mother was—and with a mind of her own, like her father."

"She won't find it easy coping with the Frasers from what I've seen," mused Carrick.

"Mhari MacLean's old enough to know what she's doing," said Shannon dourly, his pace slowing as the road continued to steepen. "It's more the Frasers I'd feel sorry for, mister."

.   .   .   .   .

Another five minutes walk, the road still twisting and climbing, brought them to the place Jimsy MacLean, sailor home from the sea, called home.

The name Ard-Tulach was carved on the rough stone pillars at the driveway entrance. Gaelic for "the high house" it was a fair description. Two storeys of solid, weather-defying grey granite with a miniature turret wing to one side, broad windows glinting in the low evening sunlight, it perched high on a fold of hillside and looked blandly on the village and harbour far below.

"I'll take that box now, mister," decided Shannon, stopping for breath before they crunched the last few yards of pebbled drive to the main door, which looked carved from solid oak. He gave a happy grunt as Carrick transferred the wedding present to his powerful, stumpy fingers. "At least we won't have to lug this with us on the way back."

Equally important, decided Carrick, the going would be downhill. He looked around for a moment. Ard-Tulach had a generous sweep of garden mainly occupied by flowering shrubs and a platoon of beehives. Several cars were parked beside the house, one of them Tara Grant's little Triumph two-seater.

But what really fascinated him was the almost unbelievable view from Ard-Tulach's frontage. The whole reef-edged length of Loch Rudha was spread below, a panoramic introduction to the open expanse of glittering, island-speckled sea beyond.

He could see a single fishing boat coming into the loch from the Minch and could just hear the faint beat of its engine. Out near the horizon, a tiny silhouette threading its way through the Passage of Tiree could only be a mailboat on the Stornoway run. Green Coll and black Staffa, even out towards Ulva—never before had he seen them in such splendour.

"Damned if I'd want to be isolated in the winter," muttered Shannon, doggedly climbing the front steps and ringing the door-bell. "And they've had trouble with the drains."

A moment passed, then a small, middle-aged housekeeper wearing a neat wrap-round overall opened the door. She had bird-like blue eyes and her hair was caught up in an old-fashioned bun, but her face beamed as she saw Shannon.

"It's yourself, Captain!" She beckoned them in, greeting Carrick with a quieter smile of his own as she closed the door again.

"What's going on, Effie?" demanded Shannon. "Those cars outside—Captain MacLean didn't tell me you were having a party."

"Och, it's just a few folk in for a wee drink before the wedding," she assured him. "They'll be gone before you eat, captain."

"Good. And we'll find our own way through. Away back to that kitchen of yours." Shannon sent her on her way with a playful slap on the backside which brought a delighted squeal of middle-aged protest.

Still chuckling, Shannon dumped the wedding present on a table in the hall then led the way along a short corridor. Opening a frosted glass door without ceremony, he led Carrick into a big, plainly furnished lounge. Almost a score of people were already in the room, scattered in groups, most of them too busy talking to notice the new arrivals. But a tall, thin man, bald and with a piratical black patch over his left eye, strode forward with an immediate, enthusiastic welcome.

"So you walked it, eh?" The voice was loud, as if still pitched against North Atlantic gales, and with a strong West Highland lilt. "Damn it, man, you could have got a car to bring you up. At your age—"

"At my age, I like the exercise. When I'm an old goat like some others, it may be different," countered Shannon with some enjoyment. "Jimsy, I brought my Chief Officer like I said—Webb Carrick. And I've warned him what to expect."

Captain Jimsy MacLean had a handshake like a steel glove, and in defiance of the other guests' more formal attire wore a rumpled tweed suit with a soft wool roll-neck sweater. His one good eye swept Carrick in swift appraisal, then he thumbed towards Shannon.

"Webb, you look like you might do me a favour. Next time you're at sea, push him over the side—somewhere deep."

"It's against regulations," said Carrick apologetically. "Otherwise I'd try to oblige."

MacLean, who looked in his middle sixties, chuckled to himself then led them over to a table laid out as a cocktail bar.

"Whisky?" Without waiting for an answer, he fished a bottle from its hiding place below the table, poured two swift, stiff measures into glasses, and handed them over. Then, just as quickly, he put the bottle back in its hiding place and explained, "My own bottle—no sense in wasting it. Now, come and meet the bride."

They followed him as he threaded his way across the room. Halfway over, Carrick saw Tara Grant. She was in black velvet trousers with a red silk shirt, and gave him a quick wave before she resumed her conversation with a couple of large, watch-chain jingling farmers.

"Here we are," said Jimsy MacLean a moment later. "Mhari, girl—here's Captain Shannon and his Chief Officer come to wish you luck."

"Captain, it's good to see you." Mhari MacLean, a pert dark-haired girl with an elfin face, wore a demure, high-collared dress of MacLean tartan. She was tall enough to have to bend a little so that Shannon could kiss her cheek. Then she eyed him with a twinkle. "Do I ask how you managed to get to Port MacFarlane when your ship should be on patrol?"

"Just luck, girl—the way things happened." Shannon made it a splutter, then remembered the rest. "There's a present for you out in the hall. Something my wife chose."

She thanked him, then it was Carrick's turn. Mhari MacLean considered him thoughtfully for a moment.

"I heard about you from Tara," she mused. "And Roddy says you helped sort out a spot of trouble on his boat this afternoon."

"More self-preservation than help," said Carrick easily. "The party was getting a little rowdy."

"There's no danger of that here." Her eyes twinkled again. "Except from my father, at any rate. Roddy's over there by the window, but he's quiet enough now."

Glancing over, Carrick understood and grinned. Pale-faced and fragile in manner, Roddy Fraser had the look of a man whose main ambition was to lie down and die somewhere. Still, somebody had managed to get him into a shirt and tie and a neatly pressed suit, leaving him more like a long-haired young accountant than the successful skipper of a lobster boat.

"There's some other people you should meet," said Jimsy Mac-Lean, nudging his elbow.

Captain Shannon had vanished into the crowd, and Carrick had to let himself be guided off on a round of introductions. One was the Presbyterian minister for the next day's wedding, another was a buxon widow named Jenny who ran the village hotel, and the district nurse was sitting sipping sherry on a couch with a thin little man who was the local freight agent. But finally his host turned him loose beside Roddy Fraser.

"Hello again," managed Fraser with a weak grin.

"At least you made it," murmured Carrick sympathetically. "Where's big brother?"

"Dan stayed back at the harbour. I'd have done the same if I'd any sense," sighed the pale-faced bridegroom. Then he remembered the man at his side. "This is Frank Farrell. He's up from London on business."

31

"Business and some pleasure, including the wedding." Farrell, in a dark blazer and slacks, nodded a greeting. "I'm more a friend of Tara Grant's—I saw you with her down at the harbour."

"And I saw you come in." Carrick sipped his drink, considering the man in close-up. Farrell's lanky good looks and long, carefully trimmed sideburns were slightly marred by an odd, thumbnail shaped scar, pocked and hairless, which sat low on his left cheek. But he looked a man who was superbly fit, and his lazy drawl still held the underlying tone of a man to whom taking decisions came naturally.

Farrell took the inspection unperturbed. He asked, "Going to be in harbour long?"

"A couple of days or so, if we're lucky." Carrick glanced around. "Brought your friend from the speedboat?"

"Dirk Peters?" Farrell shrugged. "He couldn't make it. He had to drive over to Tobermory to meet the cargo ferry due in from the mainland—it's bringing some bits and pieces he needs."

"Anyone like to swop heads with me?" interrupted Roddy Fraser miserably. He ran a sad hand across his forehead then looked at it as if expecting blood. "Man, I feel rough—and Mhari's mad as hell with me."

"That's part of the prelude to wedded bliss," Carrick told him sympathetically. He turned back to Farrell, who was grinning. "Are you staying with Peters?"

"Yes and no." The man spread his hands vaguely. "Dirk's got an old place north of here, but he sailed up aboard a motor yacht—he's putting it through a shakedown cruise before delivery to a client. She's lying in a bay along the coast and we're living aboard. There's a double benefit for me—we've been sailing around."

"Looking at islands?" queried Carrick.

"Islands and other places." Farrell pursed his lips for a moment. "Tara seems to have been talking—not that there's any real secret involved. Let's say I'm looking for potential executive hideaways."

"Plenty of islands around here," said Roddy Fraser with a determined attempt at interest. "Did you try Jimsy MacLean about Horsehead Island?"

"No." Farrell eyed him sadly. "Roddy, I'm looking for happy hideaways for clients—not places to bury them. Horsehead Island doesn't rate."

"It's a damned good spot off-shore for lobsters," flushed Fraser indignantly, then sniffed to himself. "Anyway, old Jimsy wouldn't sell. That's for sure."

"And a considerable relief," said Farrell dryly. "Do you know it, Carrick?"

Carrick did. On the charts, Horsehead Island was an uninhabited chunk of high black basalt rock lying west of Loch Rudha and a couple of miles out from the Mull coastline. *Marlin* had sailed under its shadow on several patrols and it was as bleak and desolate a spot as he could imagine.

"Well, MacLean certainly owns it," said Farrell, chuckling a little. "The story is that it used to belong to his family and he bought it back again with some of his salvage money. Call it a sentimental investment—he told me the island has been a Mac-Lean burial ground since before Noah built the Ark."

He paused, listening. A car had just come up the driveway, and had stopped outside the house, its engine revving.

"Dirk Peters," he explained shortly. "He said he'd collect me on his way back. Carrick, if you get the chance come over to see us. The boat is the *San Helena*—we'll give you the complete guided tour, and she's worth seeing."

With a farewell grin he drifted off, heading for the door. Glancing round, Carrick discovered that Roddy Fraser had settled in a chair with his eyes almost closed and a look of new-found bliss on his face. Shrugging, he stood alone and sipped his drink again.

"You don't exactly look as though you're enjoying things," said Tara Grant, suddenly appearing at his elbow. She considered him with a mild amusement. "In fact, you look downright bored."

"Not bored—just slightly lost," admitted Carrick. "This isn't exactly my scene."

"Jimsy MacLean would probably say the same. But this is a kind of duty party, mainly for people who can't make the wedding." Tara paused to smile to a couple who were leaving. "Don't despair—it's nearly over."

"It hasn't been so bad." Carrick finished his drink and laid

33

down the glass. "I was talking to Frank Farrell, and that was interesting enough. How did he start off in the property game?"

"I'm not sure. People like Frank don't usually parade their life stories," she said half-seriously. "He once tried to tell me he had a Scottish grandmother. But beyond that, about all I know is he worked abroad for a spell—somewhere in the Middle East, I think."

"And how about London?"

"We had some good times together." She looked at Carrick for a moment then shrugged. "But it didn't last long—and it didn't get serious, by mutual agreement."

The car outside blipped its engine loudly then snarled into gear. A moment later a grey, low-slung B.M.W. coupé passed the window with Farrell in the passenger seat and Dirk Peters behind the wheel. Spattering pebbles from its tyres, it travelled quickly down the driveway, stopped with a blink of brake lights at the entrance gate, then vanished out onto the road.

"Sometimes I think I should have tried harder in that direction," admitted Tara with a slightly sad sigh. "When I get round to marrying, I want somebody who won't quibble about the housekeeping money."

Carrick made a vague, answering noise. He was watching Jimsy MacLean saying goodbye to another of the departing guests. Bald head glinting with perspiration, black eye-patch as piratical as ever, the father of the bride was the picture of jovial good humour.

Until he turned away. Then there was a moment when the smile on his face sagged and he suddenly looked old and tired and strained.

Only a moment, before the previous face switched on again. But it was enough.

Carrick had seen men look that way before, men under desperate pressure. Jimsy MacLean might have found his crock of gold, might be on the brink of launching his daughter into happy matrimony—but Captain Shannon was right, something was still badly wrong.

34

To do that to a resiliently tough character with MacLean's record, it couldn't be anything small.

．　　　．　　　．　　　．　　　．

Dinner was half an hour later, in a small room at the rear of the house. The table was set for six with Jimsy MacLean at the head as host and his daughter at the other end. That left Carrick beside Tara Grant with Shannon and Roddy Fraser facing them while the housekeeper quietly came and went between courses.

Plain and simple island cooking was the pattern at Ard-Tulach, but that still meant delicately grilled salmon then, as dusk gave way to darkness outside, a main course of thick venison steaks accompanied by crisp, fresh salad. Tiny strawberries served with rich cream followed and even Roddy Fraser, who had started off with little sign of appetite, brightened considerably and took his full share.

A napkin tucked under his bearded chin, Captain Shannon beamed as a vast platter of cheese and biscuits went on the centre of the table.

"Damned if I can remember a better meal," he declared, settling back with a stifled belch. "Jimsy, you do yourself well."

"That woman Effie is a reasonable wee cook," admitted Mac-Lean, sucking his teeth. "Still remember the food in that place in Hong Kong?" He grinned. "You know where I mean, man. Where they had that Chinese girl wi' the compass in her navel. I remember you tried to—"

"Not now, dad," broke in Mhari MacLean, quickly cutting in. "I warned you—none of your usual nonsense tonight."

"It's a hell of a life when a man can't tell a story in his own house," protested MacLean, but subsided and Shannon looked relieved.

"Good." Mhari MacLean wasn't quite finished. She switched her attention to Roddy Fraser. "Talking of nonsense, how is my other hero?"

"Well—" Fraser grinned awkwardly.

"You look slightly better," she said with a chilly sweetness. "The alcoholic haze must be clearing, and that's a relief."

35

Fraser looked as if he'd like somewhere to hide as Tara joined in.

"You're right, Mhari," she agreed with a clinical frown. "The dashing groom only looks half-dead now. Pack him in ice and he might keep for quite a spell."

"Och, a man has to maintain hospitality when the wedding flag is flying on his boat," said Fraser defensively. "You know that, Mhari—it's the tradition."

"Then you've certainly done your share." Sighing, Mhari Mac-Lean thawed and wrinkled her nose at him. "All right, the wedding flag for ever—this once. But you'd better look a lot brighter in church tomorrow or people will wonder where the shotgun is hidden."

Her father chuckled, but warily. "Roddy's right about the traditions, Carrick. The wedding flag for instance—it will be hauled down in the morning, and his brother Dan will have the job of tearing it into little pieces."

"Then what happens?" Carrick sensed there was more.

"Well, all the folk who rate as their special friends, real friends, get a piece to keep—and that wee bit of cloth becomes their invitation to a free dram when this pair's silver wedding comes round." MacLean beamed across at his daughter. "Twenty-five years from now—there's a thought for you."

"Let me get through tomorrow first." Rising, she brought over a coffee pot from the sideboard. "That's enough to have on my mind. Afterwards, maybe—"

She stopped short, open-mouthed, at a sudden crash of shattering glass. It came from somewhere at the front of the house and was followed by a scream.

Next moment Jimsy MacLean was out of his chair and running from the room with Carrick at his heels. Along the hall, the front room door lay open. Inside, the room was brightly lit and MacLean's housekeeper, standing at a table piled with left-overs from the reception, was staring in horror at what was left of the front window. The main pane of glass had been smashed in, leaving a jagged framing of splinters for the black, star-crusted night beyond.

"It just happened, Captain—" the woman turned to MacLean, hands shaking as they went up to her face. "The whole window—"

"It's all right, Effie," said MacLean hoarsely, looking past her. "Steady woman, it's all right."

Going past him, avoiding the long, knife-edged shards of glass littering the carpet, Carrick stopped as a strong reek of petrol caught his nostrils. Then he saw the source—a heavy quart bottle lying broken against a chair near the window. Petrol still soaked the carpet around it—and a length of fuse-wick protruded from the bottle's neck.

Dry-lipped, he stared at the home-made fire-bomb for a moment then swung round, almost colliding with Roddy Fraser.

"Outside," he told Fraser urgently. "He's maybe still around. Move, man."

They brushed past a startled Shannon in the hall, opened the main door, and hurried down the main steps into the night.

"Where now?" demanded Fraser, still bewildered. "What's going on?"

Straining his eyes against the darkness, uneasily aware of the way they stood framed in the light from the house, Carrick shook his head.

Nothing moved among the black shadow-shapes of the garden. He could hear only the light rustle of wind among the bushes and Fraser's continued muttering by his side. But someone had thrown that petrol-bomb—someone who couldn't be far away—and who might have another of those deadly bottles ready for use.

Tight-lipped, he signalled Fraser to take the right-hand side of the driveway while he began exploring to the left. Every step, he was ready for the smash of glass and the explosion of liquid fire which might follow it.

But he found nothing and, almost glad, finally signalled Fraser again.

When they went back into the house everyone was in the front room. MacLean's housekeeper was sitting in a chair, quivering fingers laced tightly together on her lap while she made soft wail-

37

ing noises. Both girls were trying to comfort her while Jimsy Mac-
Lean stood nearby looking helpless and haggard. Shannon, however, was down on his knees beside the broken fire-bomb, his
face impassive while he examined the bottle's remains with a de-
tached, professional care.

"Well, mister?" he asked, glancing up.

"Nothing," said Carrick wryly, shaking his head. "Whoever he
was, he didn't wait."

"There wasn't much to wait for, mister." Shannon beckoned
him nearer and pointed. "I'd call this more a demonstration than
the real thing—he didn't bother to light the wick." His bearded
face twisted grimly. "But he still knew what he was doing. See
how the bottle broke, mister?"

Carrick crouched down beside him and understood. It was a
clean break, along a line which had been carefully filed round the
bottle's waist. Wordlessly, Shannon reached out a finger and
flicked at something else he hadn't noticed earlier—a small cardboard label tied round the bottle's neck with string.

The label had the simple word *Dancella* block-printed in heavy
black ink.

"Jimsy—" Shannon waited till he was sure he had MacLean's
attention "—you'd better call the police on this."

"Why?" asked MacLean in a dull voice. "You heard what Effie
said. She was in here tidying when the window was smashed in.
That's all she knows—she didn't see anyone."

"But the maniac who did it is wandering around somewhere
out there," said Shannon patiently, still on his knees. "He's got to
be found."

"No." MacLean bit his lip and half-turned away so that his
black eye-patch was towards Shannon like a shutter guarding his
emotions. "No, I—I'll let it be. It's better that way."

"Let it be?" Carrick stared at him. "Captain MacLean, do you
know what might have happened to this house—and maybe anyone in it?"

"But it didn't," answered MacLean stubbornly. "Like Shannon
says, the fuse-wick wasn't lit. It—it's probably just some fool caper

that went too far. For all I know it—well, it could be some drunk's idea of a joke because of Mhari's wedding tomorrow."

"Some joke," murmured Roddy Fraser.

MacLean ignored him. The housekeeper had fallen silent but the two girls beside her exchanged a bewildered glance of sheer disbelief.

"You can't just forget about it," protested Tara indignantly. "There's even that label and—"

"I said let it be," almost bellowed MacLean, cutting her short. "This is no affair of yours, girl. Keep out of it."

"But she's right, Jimsy," said Shannon softly. Rising, he padded across the room to face his friend—a small, determined figure who refused to be ignored. "What about that label? It says *Dancella*. Nothing else. The tanker you towed in was called the *Dancella*. Right?"

Slowly, reluctantly, MacLean nodded.

"So it might be a fool caper. Or it might not." Shannon scratched one side of his beard with a pensive forefinger. "Well, we can talk about that. But maybe we should get this mess cleared up first. You and I can do that, Jimsy. Mr. Carrick—"

"Sir?" Carrick already had an idea what was coming.

"Take another patrol around outside, just to make sure." Shannon glanced significantly at the others. "The rest of you could take that woman out of this and make her more comfortable. For a start, she looks like she could use a good stiff drink."

"Amen," muttered Roddy Fraser, and led the way towards the door.

•   •   •   •   •   •

A full fifteen minutes later, Webb Carrick leaned against the cool stonework of one of the pillars at the entrance to Ard-Tulach's driveway and wryly eyed the lights of Port MacFarlane twinkling below.

From the start, he'd been certain that he was wasting his time and that Shannon knew it. But if *Marlin*'s commander wanted to talk to MacLean alone and undisturbed, that was his business.

Even so, it still meant he'd been half-scared out of his wits when a disturbed bird had exploded out of a thick clump of perfumed broom at the exact moment he went past. Then, beyond the garden, he'd had another encounter with local wild life—this time a snarling, bright-eyed weasel which darted away into the deep shelter of the heather.

Grimacing but half-amused, he found his cigarettes and lit one between cupped hands. Then, as he took a first draw on the smoke, light, quick footsteps coming down the pebbled driveway from the house brought him round. It was Tara Grant. She had draped a black velvet jacket over her shoulders and smiled a little at him as she reached the pillars.

"I thought someone had better come and look for you." Stopping, she drew a deep breath of the night air. "Everything seems quiet enough—out here, anyway."

"It is." Something in her voice prompted him. "What about back at the house?"

"Our two captains are in the front room with the door closed. For a while back, it sounded like they were trying to see who could shout the loudest." She shrugged. "But whatever happened, it's quieter now."

Carrick grinned in the darkness. "They both like getting their own way. How's Effie?"

"Fine. We poured enough brandy down her throat to flatten a regiment—she's in the kitchen, busy telling Mhari and Roddy her life story." Tara stopped and pursed her lips, frowning. "But I—well, I just don't understand any of this, Webb. Why would anyone have a grudge against Captain MacLean?"

It was Carrick's turn to shrug. "Maybe it had something to do with that tanker, maybe not. But if that fire-bomb had been lit—"

Tara nodded soberly. "I asked Roddy where the nearest fire brigade is based. They're twenty miles away—twenty miles on these roads." She shivered, only partly at the thought, and tightened the jacket round her shoulders. "Are you staying out?"

"Not much sense in it." He eased away from the pillar. "We could see how they're getting on with Effie in the kitchen, I suppose."

"Captain Shannon might call it deserting your post." Tara chuckled a little, then shook her head. "There's a better idea. I'll show you."

Obediently, Carrick followed her back into the house. Leading the way up a broad staircase to the upper floor, she stopped to switch on another light then indicated another, narrower stairway. Remembering the turret wing, Carrick followed again till they reached a door at the top.

"In here." Opening the door, Tara let him go ahead of her into the darkened room, which was small and circular. "Now wait a moment."

Squeezing past him, she swore mildly as she bumped into something hard. Then a tiny desk-lamp clicked on and the tightly shaded beam revealed a room which left no doubts about who occupied it. The walls were hung with pictures and paintings of ships and the sea, while the shelves held closely spaced mementoes which represented a life-time afloat. Fine Eastern brasswork and African wood carvings fought for space with large, strangely shaped seashells and a small library of maritime manuals.

"Jimsy MacLean calls this his study," Tara told him with a note of amusement. "But mostly he's looking through that thing."

"That thing" was a massive, tripod-mounted Admiralty bridge telescope placed close to the room's single oval window. Going over, Carrick tried the rubber eyepiece. The view through the lens was fogged until he tightened the focus . . . then he stiffened and gave a soft whistle of surprise.

There in front of him, apparently so near he could have reached out to touch, was a dark, rippling stretch of water, a lighthouse and the black shore-line bulk of an island in the background. The lighthouse beacon flashed, he counted, and in three seconds it flashed again.

That made it Scarinish, over on Tiree. To check, he swung the telescope north on the tripod and caught the bright loom of another light—one with a slower, twelve-second flash. Suil Gorm, on the north tip of Coll, more than twenty-five miles away.

He stayed with the telescope for another couple of minutes, fascinated by how much he could see, then stepped back. Without its power, Scarinish was a mere pinprick of light far out in the night.

"Try them in daylight and it's like being up in a helicopter—Frank Farrell's description, not mine," said Tara as he turned. She had thrown her jacket on the floor and was sprawled back in an armchair. Considering him a moment, she seemed to guess what he was thinking. "I wasn't the guide that time. Jimsy was showing him around."

"I wondered," Carrick said mildly. Coming over, he perched on the desk. "How long have you been staying here, Tara?"

"About ten days. I've promised Mhari I'll help tidy the place again after the wedding then I'll have to head back to the big city —I still have to work for a living."

Carrick nodded absently. "While you've been here, how has Captain MacLean been acting?"

"Fine." She looked surprised. "Until that little business downstairs tonight, he couldn't have been friendlier. Why?"

"I'm trying to understand," said Carrick vaguely. "Ever noticed him worried or upset?"

"A couple of times, I suppose—well, maybe more than that." Tara fingered the seam of her black velvet trousers and frowned a little, as if disliking the question. "Sometimes he'll come up here and Mhari and I know to stay clear. We've made a joke of it in fact—father-of-the-bride nerves, we've called it."

"That happens." Carrick clasped his hands round one knee and leaned forward a little, the faint, musky perfume she used reaching his nostrils. "Any other possibilities?"

"Not that I know about." She shook her head firmly. "Can I have that cigarette you offered?"

He gave her one, took another for himself, and as they shared the flame from his lighter her blonde hair brushed briefly against his hand in a way that made him oddly tense.

"Something wrong?" she asked, looking up at him.

"No." Reluctantly, he went back over to the window. "Can you see Horsehead Island from here?"

"Not a chance. There's half a mountain in the way." Rising, she came over and joined him. "Why?"

"I heard it was Jimsy MacLean's family burial isle."

"That's right." She leaned against the oval window frame, then wrinkled her nose a little. "I've been out. The island is a gloomy place, umpteen generations of his branch of Clan Mac-Lean laid out in rows and the rest of it like an abandoned rock quarry. But he's very proud of it—in the old days his family were fairly important around here."

Carrick nodded. Around Mull, the name MacLean was still as common as Smith or Jones on the mainland. But only the more important families, minor chieftains at least, would rate their own burial isle.

"You know he bought it back with some of his salvage money?" Tara shook her head in wry amusement. "According to Mhari, his great-grandfather or something was forced to sell the island to bail the family out of financial trouble. But even then, they still kept the right to be buried out there."

"Who owned it last?"

"Dirk Peters, though he didn't particularly want it. Horsehead Island just happened to be part of the package when he bought that land he owns north of here—though I'll bet Dirk made a fat profit when he sold."

"Which left everybody happy." Carrick took a last draw at his cigarette then stubbed it out in one of MacLean's ornate brass ashtrays. "Maybe we should see if things are in a happier mood downstairs now."

They went back down to the ground floor. The front room door was open, the broken glass had been cleared away, and the smashed window was covered over with what looked like a piece of old canvas sail.

Shannon and Jimsy MacLean were having a drink near the window. But their faces showed that the atmosphere between them was still far from friendly.

"Where are Roddy and Mhari?" asked Tara with a deliberate cheerfulness.

"Roddy left a while back," said MacLean in a bleak voice. "He said he wanted some sleep. You'll find Mhari in the kitchen with

43

Effie." He glared pointedly at Shannon. "I'll be heading for bed myself in a minute."

"Thanks for your Highland hospitality," said Shannon dryly, finishing his drink at a gulp and setting down his glass. "I'll see you at the wedding tomorrow, Jimsy. But if you want to talk before then—"

"It's unlikely." Jimsy MacLean scowled and turned away.

. . . . .

For the first few minutes of the walk back down the hill to the harbour Shannon stayed quiet. Then, without warning, he gave a sudden, angry growl.

"Damn Jimsy MacLean for a stubborn idiot," he said bitterly. "Mister, I tried every way I could to get him to talk. All I could get out of him was a noise like a stuck gramophone record—that he'd handle any problems his own way."

"Did he admit he had problems?" queried Carrick.

"With that damned petrol-bomb through his window he couldn't very well deny it," grunted Shannon, marching on. "The salvage money he got for bringing in that oil tanker has something to do with it—and he hinted a few things have been happening to him."

"Enough to make him carry a gun?" Carrick saw Shannon's scowl deepen but went on. "I didn't see any sign of one tonight."

"No, not tonight." Shannon savagely kicked a stone ahead of him. "Just as well for him, mister. The way I felt back there, I'd have taken it and beaten him over the head with it."

They walked on in silence, reached Port MacFarlane to find only a few street lamps still burning and the houses in darkness, then, as the harbour came in sight again, Carrick slowed and glanced at Shannon. An unexpected blaze of light showed near *Marlin*'s stern and a small crowd of men were gathered on the quayside.

Hurrying on, they reached the fishery cruiser's berth and pushed their way through the muttering group of spectators. Two powerful spotlamps were blazing down from *Marlin*'s stern, trained on her launch which was idling in the water a few feet out from the quayside. Pettigrew and a couple of deckhands were aboard the launch, and a steady plume of air bubbles was rising to the surface at a spot between the small boat and the quayside.

"What's going on?" Carrick asked a fisherman, who was watching it all with a solemn interest.

"Somebody fell in, off the quay." The man shrugged at the scene below. "We'll know who it was when they get him up."

Shannon had found Jumbo Wills. When Carrick joined them, the young second mate gave a wry nod of welcome.

"Not much to tell, Webb," he said, most of his attention on the pluming bubbles. "I'd just taken over from Pettigrew when it happened—we heard a splash then a shout for help, and so did some other people though nobody saw anything. Clapper Bell's gone down to have a look."

Down below, the bubble trail from the bo'sun's scuba gear moved along then stayed stationary for a spell. Finally, the bubbles moved back towards the launch and Bell's head broke water beside it.

He went down again a moment later, carrying one end of a light line. The bubble trail returned to its previous location and, after another minute, there was a signal tug on the line and the men on the launch began to haul it in.

This time, Bell broke surface with a limp figure clutched in one arm. The launch crew hauled the body aboard, Bell clambered in after it, and the small boat nosed its way towards a flight of stone steps further along the quayside.

From there, plenty of help was available to carry the dead man up to the quay. As he was laid down and recognised, an immediate murmur of voices began.

"That's it," said one voice louder than the rest. "He was stinkin' drunk the last time I saw him—I'll bet he was tryin' to get back to his boat an' just toppled over."

"Or thought he could walk on the flamin' water," suggested someone else, with a short, brutal laugh.

They fell silent as Carrick appeared. The dead man was Andy Christie, whom he'd last seen sprawled unconscious on the Frasers' boat that afternoon. Now he lay slack-mouthed and empty eyed, long ribbon strands of dark bottom weed still clinging to his hair and water oozing from his sodden clothes.

Squelching through the crowd in his dripping scuba rubbers, Clapper Bell joined Carrick. He still had the heavy twin aqualung cylinders harnessed on his back, blood was oozing from a cut on his left hand, and he gave Carrick a twisted grin.

"There's one hell of a lot of scrap metal lying down there," complained Bell. He sucked the cut on his hand for a moment, contemplating the dead man. "That's why I needed the line—he was snagged tight on what looks like somebody's old bedstead, an' I practically had to tear him loose."

Carrick nodded. One whole side of the dead man's jacket was ripped open and his face showed a number of minor cuts and abrasions.

"Any idea who saw him last?" he asked the men around.

They exchanged glances, shrugging, then one man shoved forward.

"He was up in the village a couple o' hours back," he volunteered. "Plenty of us saw him then—that's when he had a punch-up wi' Dan Fraser off the *Razorbill*."

"And got thumped," said another man with near relish. He grinned at Carrick. "I was on the Frasers' boat the same time as you this afternoon, Chief. It was the same thing all over again—Christie lookin' for trouble and getting it."

The spotlights on *Marlin* flickered off and gradually the crowd on the quayside began to disperse. Two of Christie's crew-mates from the drifter *Anna B.* dragged a quayside, trolley over and loaded the dead man aboard. Then with Jumbo Wills as an escort, they wheeled him off towards a brick-built storeshed which doubled as Port MacFarlane's mortuary.

In the morning, the County police could drive over from Tobermory and ask their routine questions. Maybe there would be a post mortem, maybe not. . . .

Suddenly, Carrick realised he and Clapper Bell were alone and the harbour had settled down again for the night.

The bo'sun gave a massive yawn and Carrick nodded. They'd had enough for one night.

CHAPTER THREE

Webb Carrick almost welcomed the siren blast from outside the harbour. It wakened him at seven a.m. after an uneasy night's sleep. Things were always that way with him after *Marlin* had been on a rough patrol, and most of the Fishery Protection cruiser's crew would have admitted the same problem. They missed the roll and pitch of the hull, a corner of their minds felt uneasy at the general silence after the long life-blood beat of her engines. It took time to adjust again.

Yawning, screwing his eyes against the bright early morning sunshine, he climbed out of his bunk and peered through the cabin porthole. A small coaster lying off the harbour entrance blasted her siren again, demanding a berth. She was carrying sheep, a grey mass packed close together on her open foredeck, and he was glad to see a signal hoist from the harbour master's office direct her to the other side of the harbour.

Sheep meant noise and stink and flies. Probably they were on their way out to summer grazing on one of the islands, and there was money in the sheep-carrying trade. But the boats concerned earned it and most other sailors would say they were welcome.

Still yawning, Carrick washed, shaved and dressed then ambled through to the fishery cruiser's almost claustrophobically small wardroom. Jumbo Wills' place at the table showed he'd been and gone which left Pettigrew, sitting drinking coffee and scowling at a magazine.

"Not too bad a morning," said Carrick.

His only answer was a grunt, which was normal with Pettigrew. Carrick left him alone and got a grin from the wardroom steward, a round-faced man who doubled as sick-bay attendant on the strength of having once worked in a mortuary.

Breakfast was bacon and eggs, the bacon hot and crisp, the eggs still sputtering on the plate. But Carrick had barely started when the steward returned again.

"Captain Shannon says will you see him in the day-cabin, sir." The steward gave an apologetic, throat-clearing cough, which held its own warning. "He said now, sir. I'll try an' keep something for you for later."

Carrick sighed, shovelled another forkful of bacon and eggs into his mouth, and chewed it as he rose.

"Any idea what he's likely to want?" he asked Pettigrew.

"No." Pettigrew barely looked up. "I'm off watch."

"If necessary, I'll remind him," promised Carrick dryly.

He left the wardroom steward clearing away the remains of his breakfast and went along to Shannon's cabin. The door was ajar and *Marlin*'s captain was standing in the cabin in his shirt-tails, showing his small, fat hairy legs while he pressed a pair of trousers with an electric steam-iron.

"Come in." Shannon didn't bother to look up as Carrick knocked. "This is a job I want to do myself, mister. No mistakes that way."

Carrick entered the cabin and waited while Shannon finished freshening the crease on one trouser-leg then tackled the other.

"Thought I'd better wear these for the wedding," explained Shannon brusquely as he finished. "They're my best pair—usually keep them for Department half-yearly visits." Unplugging the steam-iron, he crossed the cabin and emptied its boiling water into his hated tomato plant. "Anyway, mister, I've a job for you."

"Sir?"

"The County police have been over from Tobermory—they arrived about first light." Shannon considered him with the faintly critical expression of a man whose day felt already half-gone. "You were still in your bunk, mister. But they decided they'd better have a routine post mortem on Christie's body. Those marks on his face had them worried."

"He was in a couple of fights," reminded Carrick.

"I know. And they'll probably find his blood is near proof alcohol." Shannon struggled into the trousers, fastened them, and considered the result with a scowl of disbelief. "These damned things have shrunk again. Nobody's going to tell me I've put on that much weight." He looked up quickly. "Would you, mister?"

"No, sir," said Carrick, wiping any expression from his face.

"Exactly." Shannon quickly unzipped the trousers again, gave a grunt of relief, and stepped out of them. "I want you to find the Frasers—Dan Fraser in particular. Talk to him about that second brawl and where he went and what he did afterwards."

Carrick raised an eyebrow. "Isn't that a police job?"

"They've agreed to keep it informal for the moment, because of the wedding. The odds are it will stay that way," Shannon told him with a touch of impatience. "There's another reason, mister— one you might have noticed. *Razorbill* isn't in harbour. The Frasers took her out before dawn."

"After last night?" Carrick gave a soft whistle of respect for the brothers' stamina. "I'd call that punishment."

"Or a penance," growled Shannon, scratching his shirt-tailed rump with a pensive air. "Anyway, they're not expected back till early afternoon, practically in time for the wedding. That's too late for us—go after them, mister. Take Clapper Bell along with you and use the packboat. From what I've heard, your best bet is the lobster pens in Halley Bay, not far west of here. They were planning to call in there for some reason."

He turned away, muttering over the discarded trousers. Leaving him, Carrick closed the cabin door, grimaced, and headed aft. Clapper Bell was in his usual hideaway, the scuba gear compartment near the stern. The bo'sun had a small compressor engine running and was re-charging the air tanks he'd used when recovering Christie's body.

"Five minutes an' I'll be ready, sir," agreed Bell when he heard what was planned. Then, pointing towards the racks of scuba gear, he queried, "Will we need any o' this stuff?"

"Not unless they chuck us overboard," said Carrick wryly. "And we've got to find them first. Organise the packboat, Clapper. I'm going below to see if there's any of my breakfast left."

·   ·   ·   ·   ·

The packboat, a sturdy little rubber inflatable with a forty horsepower outboard engine, creamed its way out of Port MacFarlane

49

at seven-thirty. Two children playing at the end of the harbour breakwater waved a greeting as they passed them, as Clapper Bell returned the wave, Carrick opened up the throttle.

Gathering speed, the packboat bounced and pitched its way over the light swell of Loch Rudha's dog-leg passage to the open sea then took its first drenching of spray as Carrick swung it west, keeping close to the rocky coastline. Another drenching of spray caught Bell as he tried to light a cigarette and the bo'sun gave up with a curse, tossing the sodden tobacco over the side and muttering a comment which was lost under the steady throb of the outboard.

Settled back at the tiller, Carrick gave a grin then turned his attention ahead as the little craft rounded a high point of land. A whole new stretch of the Mull coastline rolled out before them— and out across the blue water he saw the bleak, lonely bulk of Horsehead Island. That made him think of Jimsy MacLean for a moment and the puzzle of the retired sea-captain's problems.

They'd have to wait for the moment, at least till after the wedding. But once that was over . . .

"You said Halley Bay," bellowed Clapper Bell, interrupting his thoughts. "That's it to port now, if we're still goin' there."

He blinked, saw Bell was right, and steered the packboat into a sharp, pitching turn which sent the bo'sun grabbing for a handhold while another curtain of spray heavier than most soaked down on them.

The gap in the coastline was flanked by low cliffs and had broken water foaming on several patches of rock near its entrance. But it was wider than it looked and once they'd threaded past the rocks the sea died to a gentle swell. Letting the packboat's outboard engine die back to a murmur, Carrick looked around as they slowed.

Halley Bay was a small, peaceful inlet with a sandy beach. Two huts close to the shore were the only signs of human habitation, but the surface of the bay was dotted with brightly coloured floats and large rafts. There was no sign of the *Razorbill*, however, and the only other boat in sight was a small launch which had already begun heading in their direction.

"Too late or too early," grunted Clapper Bell, then gestured towards the launch. "An' that doesn't look like a welcoming committee either."

Carrick nodded. There was one man aboard the launch, an open workboat with a noisy, clattering engine, and even at that distance he didn't seem particularly friendly.

"We'll wait for him." He steered the packboat in towards the nearest of the rafts, cut the engine, and let the rubber hull drift until it bumped lightly against the big wooden outer frame.

At least a dozen similar rafts, varying in size, some constructed of wood but others supported on long, sausage-like plastic cylinders, were located in the bay. Underwater, some would be frames of slatted wood or metal, others a mixture of concrete beams and strong, close wire mesh.

Using one hand to hold the packboat against the raft, Carrick tried to guess how many lobsters were probably captive in that single pen. Depending on the pen's size and its owners' luck, the answer might be anything between five hundred and several thousand.

Lobsters had to be fresh and live for market. The pens were the modern, commercial answer, developed after long generations of keeping a few dozen lobsters in a half-sunken old boat or at best boxes which had holes drilled in them and were weighed down with stones.

"I can see some o' them," said Bell suddenly, peering over. "Think anyone would miss a few if we nicked them?"

Carrick grinned, just able to make out a few crawling, claw-groping shapes which were the top layer of the pen's contents.

"Try asking him," he told Bell, thumbing towards the launch which was now coming straight at them.

The solitary figure standing at the tiller had begun shouting and waving a fist. They waited while the other craft came nearer, the shouting and fist-waving continuing unabated. At last, the launch engine faded to an irregular, spitting cough and it came round in a slow half-circle to lie opposite them, rocking gently in the slight swell.

"Fine morning," greeted Carrick cheerfully.

"Not while you're here," came the angry, bellowed retort. The man opposite, wizened and weatherbeaten, wore faded, torn overalls and a much-darned jersey and looked in his late sixties. "Take that damned toy boat o' yours the hell out of here. This is private property—no tourists allowed."

"Who said we were tourists?" demanded Clapper Bell indignantly. "We're Fishery Protection, dad."

"Eh?" The man peered at them and showed a new disgust. "Well, I know your kind too. Keep your thievin' eyes off those lobsters, mister." He tapped his scrawny chest for emphasis. "I'm all the protection that's needed around here."

"We're looking for the Fraser brothers," Carrick told him. "Has the *Razorbill* been in this morning?"

"Here?" The wizened face scowled in suspicion. "Why do you want the Frasers, eh?"

"Our business," answered Carrick patiently. "Have they been?"

"Been an' gone." The man in the boat grinned, showing mostly bare gums. "Brought me a bottle to help make up for bein' stuck here while everybody else is havin' fun after the wedding. They're good boys, both o' them."

"So where do we find the *Razorbill* now?" demanded Clapper Bell. "Come on, dad. We just want to talk with them."

The man considered for a moment then shrugged. "Try Horsehead Island. That's where they said they were goin'—but don't blame me if they changed their minds." He sniffed derisively. "It's still supposed to be a free country."

He kept the launch where it was while Carrick started the packboat's outboard engine, then watched, still scowling, till the little inflatable had swung away and was heading out of the bay.

.　　　.　　　.　　　.　　　.

It took a full half-hour to get across to Horsehead Island. On the way, the packboat had company for a spell in the shape of a vast school of frightened, fast-travelling mackerel. Silver bodies boiling along close to the surface, lunging and jumping out of the water in their rush to escape some unseen but terrifying enemy below, they were being harried from above by squadrons of hungry, cruel-beaked gulls, white-winged killers who dived and swooped incessantly in an excited harvest.

That was how it was and always had been with the sea, a continuing carnage basic to the food needs of every living creature from the smallest of primitive organisms to the mightiest of fish. With those who escaped the natural perils just as likely to be caught in somebody's nets before the day was over.

Carrick watched the school of mackerel until they disappeared from sight, their course marked only by the following gulls. By then, Horsehead Island's tall, black cliffs were drawing near, and he leaned forward, steadying himself as the packboat lurched over a long slow swell.

"Clapper, we'll try the north-east side first." He had to shout above the outboard engine's rasping beat. "There's a landing stage round there. But keep your eyes open. They could be anywhere."

Bell grinned an acknowledgement and Carrick eased the tiller, bringing the cliffs slightly to port.

Seen close in and from sea level, Horsehead Island could hardly have been less inviting. Its sheer rock faces, some falling almost vertically to the breaking waves, were webbed with cracks and minor faults. Here and there an occasional clump of grass or perilously rooted bush managed to cling to the result, but the rest was bare and barren. Yet there was life around. As the packboat skirted round, the noise of its engine sent grey seals slithering from rock shelves and splashing into the sea while birds by the score, mostly terns and petrels, plus a few shrieking piratical skuas, rose in clouds.

Suddenly, Clapper Bell nudged Carrick and pointed. Ahead, where the sheer rock gave way to a great axe-slash of tumbled scree and giant boulders, a fishing drifter was moored close to the shore beside the thin line of a wooden landing stage. Another minute, and they saw men moving between the boat and the shore while the seabird emblem on the drifter's wheelhouse told them they'd found the *Razorbill*.

By the time Carrick brought the packboat in beside the landing stage, Roddy Fraser was there, waiting for them. He grinned a somewhat surprised greeting, caught the mooring line tossed by Clapper Bell, and quickly fastened it to a ring-bolt.

"Come visiting?" he asked as they left the boat. "I know I talked about this place, but I didn't expect a follow-up so soon."

"We want a word with Dan—maybe you too, Roddy," said Carrick easily, glancing around. Two of the *Razorbill*'s crew were stacking large wooden lobster boxes from the drifter's deck to the landing stage but there was no sign of Dan Fraser. "Isn't this your day to be bridegroom?"

"I hadn't forgotten." Roddy Fraser rubbed a wry hand along his chin. "And I'm still recovering from yesterday's caper—but we've a big air-freight order due out today, a thousand lobsters for the London market. Like my big brother says, we need the money so that's why we're here." He saw Carrick's puzzled frown and chuckled. "Come on, I'll show you."

They followed him along the creaking planks of the old landing stage then on a brief scramble across the rocks. Then he stopped and pointed.

"There's our storage base, minimum cost, maximum storage capabilities."

Just ahead, Dan Fraser and two more of the *Razorbill*'s crew were wading knee-deep round the edges of a large natural rock-pool. The pool was bottle-shaped, with a narrow neck open to the sea, and Fraser and his companions, all wearing long rubber boots, were stopping every now and again to reach down and scoop up a lobster from the bottom. As the lobsters were collected, they were placed in plastic containers hung over each man's shoulder.

"We catch them, we bring them here, and we can keep them near enough indefinitely," explained Roddy Fraser enthusiastically. "The neck to the sea is fenced off, so there's no chance of them escaping—yet we still get a full scour of fresh sea water every tide."

Nodding appreciatively, Carrick watched one of the men come out of the pool and empty the lobsters from his container into the nearest of a line of waiting wooden boxes. Lobster storage was tricky, particularly in summer—warmer water made them more active, increased their oxygen requirements, and the most common cause of storage death was literal suffocation. Even when being shipped, lobsters had to be kept damp.

"How about feeding them?" queried Clapper Bell.

"Same as the creel-pot fishers use for bait," said Roddy Fraser. "Any kind of soft bait, fish-heads, that kind of thing. They're natural cannibals too, so we've got to watch that."

He beckoned them on to the wooden boxes, many already filled with deftly packed captives, their tails bent under and claws projecting forward, legs and strange antenna twitching feebly. Picking up a lobster about eighteen inches long, he stroked a finger along its hard blue carapace shell then glanced at Carrick.

"I told you we scuba-dive for them off the island. Ever tried catching lobsters that way?"

"A few times." Carrick knew it wasn't easy. Lobsters could scuttle surprisingly quickly along the sea-bed and you had to take them from the rear, with a firm grip. Otherwise these massive claws could hand out a crushing nip which was anything but funny.

"Well, soon as we get them up we fix the claws. Some people use twine or elastic bands." Roddy Fraser tapped the lobster in his hand. "We do it the Canadian way, with a plug in the claw-joint, here."

Clapper Bell took the lobster from him and frowned at the small plastic plugs jammed into the outer edge of the claw-joints to prevent them from opening. But before he could comment Dan Fraser waded out of the storage pool and came over.

"No free samples today," he said laconically, setting down his plastic container. Brushing his long, black hair back from his forehead, he glanced quizzically at his brother. "Official visit?"

Roddy Fraser shrugged. "I haven't found out yet."

"Well, I could use a break." Dan Fraser strolled past them and sat down on a boulder. "What's up, Carrick? If this is any kind of formal inspection, you're welcome to check—just don't slow us down." He winked at them. "You wouldn't make a man miss his wedding, would you?"

"I know a few who've wished that happened," grunted Clapper

Bell. Bringing out his cigarettes, he lit one then eased back a little, leaving it to Carrick.

"We're here because of what happened at the harbour last night," said Carrick slowly. He saw Dan Fraser frown and the quick glance that passed between the brothers. "Christie's death raises a couple of questions and Captain Shannon thought—well, if we did the asking for the moment there would be fewer problems."

"A kind man, your captain," said Dan Fraser with a sardonic edge. "What kind of questions?"

"You had another brush with Christie last night." Carrick made it a statement of fact and saw Dan Fraser nod. "What happened?"

"Not much." Shrugging, the tall, long-haired fisherman traced a slow pattern on the rock with the toe of his boot. "I went ashore to get some beer when we started running out of stuff on the boat. Christie appeared and began bawling the odds about what had happened earlier, then he had a try at me with a bottle so—well, I hit him a few times." He stopped and raised an eyebrow. "What the hell does it matter anyway? The poor sod's dead now."

"Hold on," said Roddy Fraser suddenly, before Carrick could answer. His young eyes narrowing, thumbs tucked in the waistband of his khaki slacks, he glanced from his brother to Carrick. "Is anybody saying Christie wasn't drowned?"

"No. But they're holding a post mortem to be sure. And until they're sure—" Carrick left it there. "Dan, where did you go after the fight?"

"I'd hardly call it a fight," objected Dan Fraser with a wary twist of a grin. "I just hit him a few times, then booted him on his way. Afterwards—well, I got the beer and went back to the *Razorbill*. Then I stayed there. Plenty of people were aboard an' will remember—the ones that were sober enough, anyway."

"Stayed there how long?" persisted Carrick, keeping his voice friendly.

"Till after we heard someone had fallen off the quay." Dan Fraser winked at his brother. "Right, Roddy?"

Roddy nodded. "I was there when we heard. And if you want names—"

Carrick shook his head. "That's not my worry. What about you, Roddy? You left Jimsy MacLean's house—then what?"

A low growl of protest came from Dan Fraser and he heaved up from the rock.

"Easy, now," said Clapper Bell softly, the cigarette still glued between his lips. "We're tryin' to do you two a favour, remember?"

"Some favour. But I don't mind," declared Roddy Fraser cheerfully. "Dan, you're going to have to forget the big brother act—hell, I'll be a married man in a few hours' time. Relax, will you?"

Still scowling, Dan Fraser subsided again.

"Well?" asked Carrick quietly.

"I said goodnight to Mhari and got out before midnight—she's superstitious about a bride seeing her 'groom before church on the wedding day. Then, the way my head was still feeling, I wandered along the shore for a spell on my ownsome—but I was still back aboard the *Razorbill* before we heard someone had gone in."

"Half an hour back," interjected Dan Fraser quickly.

"Uh-huh." Roddy Fraser grinned but shook his head. "Five, maybe ten minutes. No more—but I'd say it's enough."

"It sounds that way to me," agreed Carrick with some relief. He checked his wrist-watch then glanced at Clapper Bell. "Time we were heading back to Port MacFarlane, before the Old Man sends out search parties."

"Well, if you're satisfied—" Dan Fraser thawed a little "—look, we're having a coffee break soon. Stay for a cup."

His brother nodded. "And while you're here, take a wander up and see why old Jimsy MacLean makes such a fuss about this place. You might be surprised."

Carrick hesitated. There was no real need to get back, the day was fine and warm, and he was curious in more ways than one about this strange, bleak outpost of rock. He glanced at Clapper Bell and waited for his reaction.

"I'll settle for the coffee an' a look around here," declared the bo'sun, still eyeing the lobsters hopefully.

Nodding, Carrick left him watching the brothers start work

57

again. Walking along, he found a rough path which wound its way upward from the shore and followed it.

Clearly defined, the path quickly steepened and he plodded on, telling himself how much more difficult it must be any time mourners came the same way but carrying a coffin on their shoulders to the MacLean burial ground above.

A last few scrambling steps to the top left him gasping for breath. Then he stopped, glad the climb was over—and fascinated at what it revealed.

He was on a small, absolutely flat plateau covered in wind-stunted gorse and heather. It was a place of silent, almost eerie isolation, looking out on one side towards Mull and the misty peaks of mainland Scotland and on the other towards a wide scatter of islands in a blue carpet of sea flecked by the white tips of breakers.

All against a sky which had only a few wisping clouds to break its serenity . . . there could be other moods in such a place on other days, but Carrick suddenly found it easy to appreciate why some long-dead clan chieftain had wanted Horsehead Island as his final resting place. And why his descendants right up to the present could feel the same.

The little path led on through the gorse and heather to a small hollow guarded by a rough, dry-stone wall. He went through a narrow gap in the wall and into a tiny graveyard almost choked by vegetation. Timeworn headstones, a few cracked or broken, at least one fallen on its side, marked the last resting places of generations of MacLeans.

One small group of stones, much older than the rest, still retained faint traces of elaborate Celtic carving. Others were new enough to mark the graves of people Jimsy MacLean might have known in his childhood.

Leaving the place, Carrick went over to the edge of the little plateau. Picking up a stone, he tossed it over the edge and watched its long fall to the sea.

Then he went back down the path towards the landing stage.

Lounging on the deck of the *Razorbill*, most of them stripped to the waist and enjoying the sun, the Fraser brothers and their crew were gossiping with Clapper Bell when Carrick reached them. As he climbed aboard, Dan Fraser filled another mug from a blackened coffee pot and passed it over.

"Find the place?" he asked.

Carrick nodded and sipped the coffee, which was heavily sugared. "That's quite a view up there."

"It's a damned wild spot in winter, believe me." Roddy Fraser stretched luxuriously and yawned. "Well, the way things are going another hour or so should see us finished here."

"If we keep working." His brother signalled the other men. "On your feet, lads. We'll be along directly."

The crewmen rose reluctantly but headed off. Lighting a cigarette, Carrick watched them head back towards the lobster pool then turned to the Frasers again.

"It's bad luck you had this order for today," he commented.

"Well, it's money—" Dan Fraser gave a soft chuckle "—och, and I'll let you into a secret, one even Roddy doesn't know yet. The order isn't due for delivery until tomorrow, but I had a notion we wouldn't be in much of a state to be filling it then."

"You crafty basket," said his brother, startled. "You mean you've had me sweating my guts out here—"

"Easy now," soothed Dan Fraser, stopping him. "It makes sense —this way, the lads can enjoy tonight without any worries about working tomorrow."

"Does it make sense for the lobsters?" countered his brother.

"No problems there either," declared Dan Fraser cheerfully. "When we get back to Port MacFarlane we'll give the boxes a real damping down then get them on the truck for the airstrip as usual. They'll keep fine till they're air-freighted out tomorrow."

"All right." His brother nodded bitterly. "Dan, if there was money involved you'd work your granny till she dropped. And if I'd known, I'd have told you to go to hell—I'm supposed to be skipper on this damned boat."

"But I've got that worry for the next couple of weeks," reminded Dan Fraser, chuckling.

"Air freight must put your costs up," mused Carrick. "How do you balance it?"

"Guaranteed top quality supplies that fetch top quality prices," answered Roddy Fraser. "We give same-day delivery—" he scowled briefly "—or we're supposed to, anyway. That way, we catch markets the other boats can't touch with their old road and rail shipment methods, and we get practically no deaths in transit."

"Roddy's idea, and it works," completed Dan Fraser happily.

Carrick nodded. "But why store your catches out here? Why not use Halley Bay, like the other boats?"

"Because this island is where we do most of our fishing," said Roddy Fraser patiently. "Anyway, you're wrong—we do use the bay a little. We've a small lobster pen there with stock we've been nursery rearing for months, a sort of reserve supply—an old character named Francie MacPhee keeps an eye on them for us."

"We met him," grunted Clapper Bell, who'd been sprawled on his back, almost forgotten. "His idea of a welcome is to damned nearly ram you."

"That's his job, to be a kind of general watchman," said Dan Fraser with a grin. "He's paid by all the boats who use Halley Bay." He got to his feet and signalled his brother, who also rose. "We'd better get back and give our lads a hand."

Carrick and Clapper Bell followed their example and, leaving the drifter, walked back along the landing stage towards the packboat.

"See you in church," said Roddy Fraser as they parted.

"If it doesn't fall around our ears first," suggested his brother dryly. "Last time I was in one, I hadn't started shaving."

.   .   .   .   .

There was a new arrival in harbour when the packboat returned to Port MacFarlane. The coaster had gone, and her berth had been taken by a large, white motor yacht which dwarfed most of the fishing boats.

Webb Carrick had guessed she was the one Frank Farrell had talked about even before he saw the name *San Helena* in gold lettering across the square-cut stern. Motor yachts her size were few and far between along their stretch of the coastline. Some seventy feet long and around sixty tons gross, she had a raked bow and smoothly stepped superstructure. From the tinted glass on her saloon deck to the big, luxury fishing chairs at her stern every line hinted at a design which combined ocean cruising power and penthouse style living, with a crew of paid hands to do the work.

Clapper Bell was at the packboat's tiller and brought her round to pass close to the San Helena's berth. As they admired her lines a voice hailed them and, looking up, Carrick saw Frank Farrell grinning down from the yacht's high cockpit bridge.

"How do you like her?" hailed Farrell. "Any bids?"

"What would I do with a floating gin palace?" Carrick called back.

Farrell laughed, and Dirk Peters appeared beside him.

"Pay us a visit later, Chief Officer," invited Peters. "Maybe I could end up selling a couple like her to Fishery Protection. It's time you had some decent transport."

The packboat steered away again—and Clapper Bell had a scowl on his face.

"Ruddy pansified week-end sailors," he muttered, half to himself. Giving the tiller an unusually vicious twitch, he sniffed hard. "Maybe that gold-plated tub looks fast, but Marlin could give her a head start in any sea an' still leave her looking sick. Hell, they've probably got fitted carpets in the flamin' heads."

Which was as near a speech from the burly Glasgow-Irishman as Carrick was ever likely to hear.

Two minutes later they were back aboard the fishery cruiser. Leaving Bell to supervise the packboat's being brought aboard again, Carrick went in search of Captain Shannon and met him emerging from the radio room.

"You took your time, mister—as usual." Shannon beckoned him to follow and led the way along to his day-cabin. Inside, he closed the door and waved Carrick into a chair, listening to his report with minimal interest.

"In other words, both the Frasers are in the clear," he nodded as Carrick ended. "That's if there is anything to worry about—the County police were round again and seem satisfied enough."

61

Crossing the cabin, he stirred the papers on his desk in absent fashion then looked up. "I've done one thing about the Jimsy MacLean business, mister. There's a signal on its way to the Department asking them to check through the reports on that oil tanker's salvage."

"You think there might have been something odd about it?" queried Carrick.

"I don't think anything yet," snapped Shannon. "But I damned well want to find out."

"And if there is?"

"Then I'll personally take Jimsy by the throat until he talks some sense." Shannon drew a deep breath then let it out as a sigh. "For the moment, what matters is we're due at the church at seventeen hundred hours, mister. Report here at sixteen-thirty if you want a drink first—and you're liable to need it."

* * * * *

Jumbo Wills was with them when they went ashore minutes before the seventeen hundred hours deadline. Pettigrew had volunteered to remain aboard as watch-keeping officer—he didn't like weddings and said so with the kind of intensity which had to be forged from bitter personal experience.

Other figures were heading for the church from boats all over the harbour. Fishermen in their heavy black Sunday best suits, uncomfortable in tight white shirts and ties, marched determinedly and shouted greetings to friends as they passed. Several car-loads of guests from other parts of the island came rolling in, farmers and their families. The villagers were going too—not a shop in Port MacFarlane was open, wives in bright cotton dresses and floppy hats bought on their annual visit to the big city trailed husbands and offspring along, giving their menfolk an extra tug and a warning glare as they passed the large canvas marquee which had somehow sprung up in a field just behind the village hotel.

The marquee's turn would come later. A couple of beer trucks were unloading the last of their supplies, and a harassed barman was busy tacking up the signs which said Men and Women— probably hoping he had them pointing in the right directions.

62

The church, when they reached it, was small and already crowded. But Captain Shannon bored a way through, Carrick and Jumbo Wills sticking close behind, and somehow they ended up in a pew surprisingly near to the front.

"How long should this last?" asked Jumbo Wills out of the corner of his mouth. He glanced round at the tiny stained-glass windows which depicted fishing scenes and the stone memorial tablets, almost all to fishermen lost at sea, which peppered the walls. "Webb, I don't know about you, but this kind of thing makes me nervous."

Carrick grinned. "Worried about that redhead back at Oban?" he murmured.

The second officer's freckled young face flushed a brick red. The girl at Oban had been down at the quay to wave goodbye on each of their last three trips. But a warning growl from Shannon and the wheeze of the pedal-operated church organ starting up saved him from having to reply.

Strikingly beautiful in a gown of white, hand-embroidered lace, Mhari MacLean came confidently down the aisle on her father's arm. Jimsy MacLean wore a kilt which smelled of mothballs as he passed, and behind them, sole bridesmaid but with a couple of tiny flower-girls in tow, Tara Grant was in pastel blue silk with a tiny matching hat almost lost under her blonde hair.

In front of the altar, beside the minister, Roddy Grant and his brother stood stiffly in hired morning suits. There was a brief shuffling into position, the organ faded with a wail, and the service began.

As island weddings went, it was a reasonably short service—only an hour and twenty minutes by Carrick's watch. Even at that, the father of the bride was openly fidgeting before it was halfway through and several of the congregation were beginning to yawn.

But the minister, an Old Testament fire-and-brimstone preacher in the Free Kirk style, ploughed on relentlessly. He had determined to make the most of one of the few chances that came his way to scorch the tails of so many back-sliding, normally absent

63

parishioners. His sermon's theme was sin, and by his personal reckoning Port MacFarlane seemed to wallow in every kind ever catalogued plus a few more all its own.

In between times, Mhari MacLean and Roddy Fraser were somehow married. At last, the organ wheezed a final triumph and they came back down the aisle as man and wife. After a moment's pause, friends, relatives and gawpers alike began a scrambling rush to escape back out into the open.

There, the little churchyard held an uncertain, milling mob of people while the bridal party posed and the inevitable cameras clicked. Then came a sudden loud skirl of bagpipes and the crowd parted.

In Port MacFarlane, a wedding march meant just that. First came two pipers, one in Fraser tartan and the other in MacLean tartan, striding mightily and blowing in resolute style, the sunlight glinting on the clan badges in their bonnets and the heavy silver brooches which secured their shoulder-slung plaids. Then the bride and groom, Mhari's veil thrown back from her face and Roddy grinning like a schoolboy, were followed by Tara Grant and Dan Fraser, with Jimsy MacLean and a scatter of relatives trailing.

The guests followed, a long crocodile of cheerfully jostling humanity whose tail was still leaving the churchyard when its head arrived at the marquee behind the village hotel.

"Every man for himself now, mister," rumbled Captain Shannon, and began elbowing his way in Jimsy MacLean's direction. In the next few seconds Carrick was swept into the marquee and lost all trace of Jumbo Wills. Trod on by a large woman with a MacLean sash across her ample bosom, he miraculously surfaced near the bar and had a drink shoved in his hand.

"Survival of the fittest," said a voice in his ear. He turned and found himself facing Frank Farrell. The property agent, immaculate in a grey lightweight suit, raised his eyes despairingly. "Why can't they settle for a nice, peaceful riot. Dirk Peters was with me a moment ago and—"

"And I'm back." Peters shoved through to join them, a drink in each hand. He greeted Carrick with a twisted grin on his

64

square, broken-nosed face, a dark stain spreading down his smartly cut blazer. "I was rammed by a fishing boat skipper and his beer. Chief Officer, if we survive this, remember the invitation to the *San Helena* is still open."

Carrick had time to nod and then they were gone. In the middle of it all, somewhere, there was a wedding cake and a queue to kiss the bride but the pressure didn't ease until a blast of amplified pop music signalled the start of dancing outside the marquee where a floor of wooden planks had been laid.

He claimed Tara Grant there, rescuing her from a vast, sweating, tweedy farmer and, when the music stopped for a moment, they retreated to the edge of the crowd. Around them, jackets were being discarded and wedding finery was starting to wilt. He spotted Jumbo Wills, working energetically on a petite redhead, then saw Shannon clinking glasses with a beaming Jimsy Mac-Lean.

"My feet are killing me," complained Tara. Clinging to his arm, she eased off her shoes and gave a murmur of relief. "Webb, I'm soft and city-bred—if I survive all this it's going to be a miracle."

But she let Dan Fraser take her back on the wooden boards a few minutes later and the next Carrick saw of her she was laughing and joking with Dirk Peters. After that she vanished and Carrick, claiming the little redhead from Jumbo Wills for a dance purely to annoy him, suddenly realised that it was already dusk overhead. Pressure lamps began throwing bright pools of light and soon it was night.

Then Tara returned. She had changed into a sweater and trousers and reached him just as the music stopped and the bagpipes began skirling again.

"Roddy and Mhari's going-away time," she explained, shouting in his ear. "They've a sail-boat in the harbour."

Bride and groom appeared a moment later, also in sweaters and trousers and escorted by Dan Fraser. This time the procession that followed them was a shouting, laughing mob who danced and sang down the main street of the village—and at

65

the harbour they gathered round a flight of stone steps which led down to a tiny motor sailer with a midships cabin and an open cockpit at the stern.

Dan Fraser went aboard with the couple for a moment, then jumped ashore and cast off its mooring lines. Engine a muted throb, the motor sailer eased away from the quay to more shouts and cheers with Mhari waving from the tiller and Roddy Fraser already unfurling the mainsail.

The crowd cheered again as a surprise cluster of rockets burst in the sky above the harbour, fired from a couple of the fishing boats. Then, as the motor sailer eased past Port MacFarlane's breakwater and began heading down the loch, they gradually began drifting back towards the marquee's renewed music.

"Off duty now, Tara?" asked Frank Farrell, appearing out of the shadows beside them.

"Off duty—and exhausted," she confirmed, laughing. "Where's Dirk?"

"On the *San Helena*." Farrell thumbed towards the long, pale silhouette further along the harbour. "How about bringing Carrick over for a drink with us?"

"Webb?" She glanced at Carrick quizzically. "They might even let us sit down somewhere."

Carrick felt that way too. They followed Farrell's tall, thin figure over to the motor yacht's berth and went aboard. The stateroom cabin was brightly lit and inside its door they both stopped, Carrick whistling a soft appreciation.

He'd expected luxury but not quite on such an opulent scale. Skin rugs covered much of the polished teak of the deck, there were shaded lights, deep leather armchairs, even paintings on the bulkhead walls. Standing behind a miniature, well-stocked bar, Dirk Peters had his jacket off and already had a glass in his hand.

"You look like refugees," he said dryly. "Well, the crew's ashore somewhere, so it's strictly do-it-ourselves if you want anything more than a drink."

"A drink seems fine." Tara flopped in a chair and kicked off her shoes. "Something long and cool, Dirk. That's the way I feel."

Peters chuckled throatily. "Carrick?"

"Beer if you have it."

"The *San Helena* has everything—it's a rule we made," Farrell told him while Peters got busy behind the bar. "That's the best of having a borrowed boat."

"I'm paying the wage-bill," protested Peters, coming round with the drinks in record time. "I've a grateful seller down south who couldn't afford to run her any more, and an equally grateful buyer who still has to find that out the hard way—neither of them is worried about me taking a little holiday. That's fair, isn't it, Carrick?"

"He's just a plain, simple sailor—" Tara grinned across at Carrick then took her glass "—or so he says. What do we drink to, anyway?"

"Island weddings," suggested Farrell with a sardonic grimace. "Heaven preserve me from another."

"It's just warming up," mused Carrick, sipping his beer and finding it was cold enough to leave the imprint of his hand on the glass. "How about the happy couple? Where are they sailing to, Tara?"

"Nowhere special. Roddy wants to wander their way up the islands for a couple of weeks." Tara wrinkled her nose. "Well, it's a nice idea but I'd probably get sea-sick." She turned her attention to the other men. "How long are you two staying here?"

"Another week, though we'll be cruising most of the time," Peters told her. Going back to the bar, he freshened his own drink then added over his shoulder, "Don't let the trimmings fool you, Carrick—I've got to work for a living. So does Farrell."

"And I've more or less finished up here," nodded Farrell, frowning a little. "Stay away from base too long and you're dead in the property game." He glanced at Peters. "How about showing Carrick over the boat while he's here?"

Tara didn't want to move. They left her curled up in the chair and Dirk Peters led the way.

By the time the next twenty minutes was over, Webb Carrick was sadly aware he'd been born into the wrong league.

Like Clapper Bell had forecast, the *San Helena* had fitted carpets into the heads. The washbasin and bath in the owner's private suite had gold-plated taps and the rest of her passenger areas had luxury to match.

But she also had two big turbo-charged diesels of around six hundred horsepower which gave her a twenty knots cruising speed and almost every automated aid it would have been possible to get aboard. On the upper cockpit bridge it could all be controlled from a single bucket seat facing a leather-bound steering wheel and a set of switches no more complicated than those in a sports car's dashboard.

"She's a good sea-boat too," emphasised Peters as they headed back to the main stateroom to collect Tara. "Carrick, I'd put even money on her being easier to handle in rough weather than anything else you'll find around this coast—including your fishery cruiser."

"Keep your money in your pocket, Dirk," murmured Farrell. "I don't see Fishery Protection taking side-bets."

Carrick could only shrug. He'd been impressed. But like Clapper Bell, he had his own opinion.

．　　　．　　　．　　　．　　　．

He left the motor yacht with Tara by his side a few minutes later and they walked along the stone-slabbed quayside in silence for a spell. Then, as they reached the start of the village street, the lights and music of the wedding celebration on ahead, Carrick stopped.

"Want to go back there?" he asked quietly.

"I should." She eyed him quizzically in the pale moonlight then gave a slight headshake. "Not unless you do."

They turned and went the other way, along a path which led down to the shore. There, the sand crunched lightly beneath their feet and the soft murmur of the sea was very close. Oystercatchers and terns were chorusing along the water's edge, their shrill cries oddly peaceful. They walked a little further, then stopped again and he kissed her.

Tara's lips were gentle, moist and welcoming. When he kissed her again, her body warm and close against his own, they answered the only question remaining.

The sand was cool and dry and soft as it became their total world against the background murmur of the sea.

CHAPTER FOUR

It was three a.m. when Webb Carrick returned to *Marlin* and even then singing and music were still coming from the celebrations in the village.

Going aboard the fishery cruiser, he returned the yawning salute of the leading hand on gangway watch. The man reported all but two of the leave party had returned and the implication that Carrick was among the stragglers was left unsaid.

In his cabin, he undressed slowly then smiled. Through the porthole, the hill above Port MacFarlane was a black bulk against the night sky with the village a twinkle of lights at its foot. Captain Shannon had promised him an island wedding was something to remember but even Shannon couldn't have guessed how true that had turned out.

Almost as soon as he lay down on his bunk he was asleep.

And it was the insistent, penetrating yowl of *Marlin*'s 'tween decks alarm klaxon that jerked him awake again. Grey dawn showed through the porthole and the fishery cruiser's big twin diesels were already coughing to life.

It was six a.m. by his watch. Scrambling into a sweater and slacks as the klaxon died, Carrick pulled shoes on his bare feet and dived from the cabin towards the bridge. Other feet were scurrying along *Marlin*'s decks and he heard the clattering rumble as her gangway was pulled aboard.

Captain Shannon was already on the bridge when he got there. The soft red night-patrol lights showed the small, plump figure was still wearing pyjamas, the trousers stuffed into seaboots and a duffel coat draped over his shoulders. The helmsman and a petty officer were in their places, a tousled Jumbo Wills arrived seconds later, and out on deck he saw Pettigrew running towards the bow lines.

"We're going out, mister," Shannon told him curtly, hoisting himself into the command chair. "God knows where eventually, but the trouble's at Halley Bay. The lobster pens have been raided, some old watchman thumped on the head and half the pens hauled out to sea." He swore bitterly into his beard. "Lobster rustlers—well, there's a first time for everything. So don't just stand there with your mouth open. Move, mister."

All over *Marlin* lights flickered and figures bustled as she came to rapid life in the grey half-light. Carrick saw his own check-list completed on the bridge, called the engine room on the intercom, then hung up and turned to Shannon.

"Ready to leave harbour, sir."

Shannon nodded. "Bow lines, Mr. Wills."

"Sir." Wills signalled forward from the bridge wing. There was a brief flurry of movement near the bow, then a quick torch-flash. "Bow lines clear, sir."

"Stern lines. Engine room stand by."

Shannon kept them fully occupied for the next couple of minutes as the fishery cruiser's engines gently eased her away from the quayside. She turned slowly in the harbour's narrow confines, gradually gathering pace as she headed out.

"Half ahead both, mister," ordered Shannon as the long, low shape of the breakwater slid past in the gloom.

"Half ahead, sir." Carrick flicked the telegraph and the diesels responded with an immediate increase in beat. He glanced at Shannon, saw the angry set of the bearded face in the red glow, but still asked, "How much do we know?"

"Damned little," said Shannon curtly. "I've a signal that the County police are on their way by road. But they've a long drive —we'll be there first." He sucked his lips bitterly. "Mister, this really lands us in it. Just one of those rafts can hold lobsters worth up to ten thousand pounds in anybody's money!"

Jumbo Wills, waiting on the bridge wing, gave a surprised whistle then fell silent under Shannon's glare. Coming in, Pettigrew sensed the atmosphere and stayed in the background.

"Halley Bay first, then a general search pattern and full radar scan." Shannon beat a fingertip tattoo against the command chair. "Helmsman, wake up. You're two full points off course, man."

Easing the wheel, the helmsman frowned apologetically. "She seems sluggish, sir."

"I know what's sluggish around here," snarled Shannon. "Keep your wits about you."

Bow wave increasing and her white wash spreading astern, *Marlin* headed on down Loch Rudha's narrow, difficult passage to the sea. Shannon peered ahead, almost ignoring the radar and sonar checks, watching the land still forming on either side in the dawn light, using instinct and memory to calculate when his ship would need to make the dog-leg turn to clear the main band of reefs ahead.

"This watchman at Halley Bay," he said suddenly. "Francie somebody—"

"Francie MacPhee," nodded Carrick. "He's an aggressive little character."

"Well, he was on the receiving end this time." Shannon gave a sound like a dry chuckle. "They left him tied up and cut the 'phone wire from his shore station. But he sounds a tough old bird. He got free, hiked to a farm, and 'phoned the police from there. Now—well, whatever is towing those rafts can't have got far."

That had been on Carrick's mind. From what he'd seen, the lobster rafts would be nightmare things to tow. But they might not have been taken far. Lying almost level with the water in their ordinary state, they would be easy enough to hide—almost invisible until a whip was almost on top of them.

The intercom 'phone buzzed and Carrick answered it. The radio room had received a routine weather report. He told them it could wait, and hung up.

"Starboard helm, full rudder," ordered Shannon a moment later.

"Starboard full, sir." The helmsman swung his wheel and the

73

fishery cruiser's bow came round obediently, heading away from a long patch of broken white water ahead. "She's still sluggish, sir."

"Then compensate, man." Shannon kept his eyes ahead, counting under his breath. "Midships now."

"Midships." The helmsman shifted his grip on the spokes, seemed to struggle with the wheel for a moment, then suddenly it spun free, like a child's toy. He stared round and blurted, "She's not answering. Telemotor gear must have packed in. I—"

Bouncing down from the command chair, Shannon shoved him aside and tried for himself. The steering wheel was slack and useless. Still answering full starboard rudder, *Marlin*'s bow was continuing to swing and they were heading in a fifteen knot curve towards another line of foam marked rocks—the other side of the dog-leg channel.

"Sir—" began Jumbo Wills.

"Shut up," snapped Shannon. There was no time to switch to hand steering gear, not enough distance to even attempt to manoeuvre on engines alone. He bit his lip for an instant then spat out the only order remaining. "Emergency full astern both."

Slapping the telegraph levers, Carrick could picture the startled reaction below. But like every other man on the bridge he could only stand helpless, watching that line of rock coming rapidly nearer while *Marlin* drove on.

Seconds passed, then suddenly the beat of the diesels gobbled and changed to a protesting roar. The deck underfoot shuddered and the whole ship vibrated as if ready to fall apart while the twin screws bit and thrashed the water in full reverse power.

But six hundred tons of steel takes a lot of stopping and the fishery cruiser's shallow draught and smooth-lined hull were for once her worst enemies. The line of rock kept looming, individual fangs now discernible among the foam and eddies, while a new sound, the tortured scream of bearings, rose above the thunder of exhaust from *Marlin*'s squat stack.

It was having effect. The fishery cruiser was visibly slowing. But it wasn't going to be enough. Giving Carrick a small, despairing headshake, Shannon stayed where he was with his hands knuckle-tight on the useless wheel. Behind them, Pettigrew had the alarm klaxon braying a final warning throughout the ship—and still slowing on her starboard curve, *Marlin* struck.

Steel plates grated loudly on rock, a massive quiver ran through the hull, the deck canted even more to starboard, and obscure, mysterious clatters and crashes came from below. As it ended, Carrick slammed the bridge telegraph levers to "Stop Engines."

The tortured diesels died with a moan. They were left with the steady breaking of the waves on the rocks, the hum of the bridge electronics and a monotonous groaning noise from for'ard as the damaged hull rubbed the rock with each new swell.

Carrick looked around. Jumbo Wills had been thrown to the deck and was picking himself up, unhurt. The duty petty officer had a gash on his forehead where he'd been hurled against a metal stanchion. Pettigrew and the helmsman were intact.

But Captain Shannon was still clutching the wheel, face stricken, shoulders slumped, a man suddenly shrivelled and aged.

"Sir." Carrick touched him on the shoulder.

"Carry on," said Shannon hoarsely, without looking.

"Aye, aye, sir," said Carrick with a deliberate formality. He knew Shannon wasn't the kind to thank anyone for sympathy, and right then the fishery cruiser's injuries amounted to an almost physical hurt to her commander.

He stepped back, told the helmsman to help the dazed petty officer down to sick-bay to have the bloodied gash on his head fixed, then turned to Pettigrew and Wills.

"Get the damage control party for'ard," he told Pettigrew shortly. "Report back here as soon as you can."

The older man nodded and was on his way.

"Jumbo, several things for you." He beckoned Wills out on the bridge wing. In the brightening light, their plight would be clear to any boat moving in the Loch Rudha channel, but the fishery cruiser still amounted to a navigational hazard. "Regular 'vessel aground' warning signals first—then make a flag hoist, R and U. Station a man aft with red flares too, just in case."

"Right." Wills frowned along the deck, his young freckled face

75

twisted in concern. The R and U flags were international for danger and the need to pass with care. "How bad do you think this is?"

"Ask me once Pettigrew gets back," Carrick suggested impatiently. "Tell Clapper Bell I want two sets of scuba gear readied. Then do a full ship's round, all departments, but don't waste time."

The bridge intercom 'phone buzzed. Crossing over, he scooped up the receiver and answered.

"What the hell's been goin' on?" crackled the peeved voice of Andy Shaw, their engineer. "First you knock hell out o' my diesels, then everything down here gets thrown in the air—an' never as much as a word to explain."

"Are your feet still dry, Andy?" asked Carrick wearily.

"Aye, but—"

"Then stop worrying and do something useful. The telemotor steering gear packed in. I want to know why."

He hung up, heard an odd chuckle from behind, and turned to find Captain Shannon standing beside him. Wills had gone, they were alone in the bridge, and though Shannon's face was still grey and his lined eyes held a bitter anger there was purpose back in his manner.

"That's the way to tell them, mister," said Shannon gruffly. "But I'll take over now. That bit about the scuba suits—external check?"

Carrick nodded.

"Go ahead." Shannon sighed a little. "I've something of my own to do—a signal to Department telling them we're stuck here. That'll make a good start to somebody's day."

"Sir." Carrick hesitated.

"I'm all right, mister," said Shannon, shaping a scowl. "Any time I need a mother hen for a first officer, I'll let you know."

Which meant things were as near back to normal as mattered.

•   •   •   •   •

Five mintues later he and Clapper Bell were ready. Though it was going to be shallow water work, both wore black neoprene rubber "wet" suits and full scuba gear.

The "wet" suits, which admitted a thin layer of water between the rubber and the wearer's body then let trapped body heat provide its own insulation, always made sense in the chill waters of the Scottish coast. Admiralty tables showed cold water could reduce body efficiency by up to forty per cent.

The rest was standard, regardless of circumstance. Quick-release weight belt, knife in its leg sheath, depth gauge, rubber-sealed compass and compact deflated life-vest, flippers and face-mask. Carrick snugged the big heavy-duty twin-cylinder aqualung harness a fraction higher on his shoulders, saw Clapper Bell do the same, and nodded.

Face-masks down, breathing tubes gripped between their teeth, they crossed the deck to where a section of rail had been removed and went over backwards into the slapping waves.

From there, they duck-dived down beneath the surface. Conscious of the slow, familiar pulse-beat click of his demand valve, clearing his ears as they numbed momentarily, Carrick looked round, saw Clapper Bell and the fine trail of bubbles feathering from the bo'sun's aqualung, then signalled.

Together, they finned towards the stern. A few small fish darted from their path and long fronds of marine weed waved like a forest below. But Carrick's eyes were on the long, dark line of the fishery cruiser's hull. He stopped beside her useless rudder, still jammed in that fatal starboard turn, glanced at the motionless propellers above, then signalled Bell again.

They went back the way they'd come. There was deep water free from obstruction all the way under *Marlin*'s hull until the final few feet before her bow. Then the reef began, rising from the bed of the loch like some strange undersea fortress.

Carrick winced at the rest. *Marlin* had scraped over a first line of reef then had rammed hard into a second, slightly higher barrier, smashing a way through before being stopped. Broken rock was jammed against her heavily scored plating, which was visibly buckled. Clapper Bell tapped his shoulder and pointed. To their right a large, flat-headed conger eel lay almost cut in half, still writhing in a slow, final death agony and disturbing a cloud of bottom sediment.

Going on, they eased their way carefully over the broken rock while the wavering light from above showed them that *Marlin* had still been lucky. The way she'd jammed had stopped her from what might have been final execution, a new, sharp-fanged series of ridges which rose in tiers towards the surface.

But she was still stuck fast, and low on the starboard bow a chisel-edged outcrop of rock had holed the hull but remained there, intact, like a cork in a bottle.

A final check, and Carrick pointed upwards. They finned towards the surface, emerged near where they'd gone in, and were helped aboard.

"Not what I'd call clever," declared Clapper Bell once he'd spat out the breathing tube and shoved back his face-mask. Water still dripping from his suit, he wiped a hand across his nose and sniffed hard. "We could blast some o' that rock away, but the Old Man's still goin' to need a tub to get us clear."

When Carrick made his report on the bridge, however, Captain Shannon preferred to be optimistic.

"We're taking water, mister, but so far nothing the pumps can't handle. Pettigrew's damage control squad are starting temporary repairs, we grounded at low water so we've the tide on our side when it comes to refloating. No, we'll give it a try on our own at next tide and that gives us plenty of time to ready."

The pumps were already throbbing and throwing steady white plumes of water from the fishery cruiser's hull. But something else caught Carrick's eyes. *Marlin*'s cutter was being swung out from the boat deck.

"I'm sending Wills and a boat's crew to Halley Bay," said Shannon in explanation. "We need some kind of presence there, and for the moment that's all they're likely to get. I radioed Department and there's a signal back—the nearest cruiser that could take over is *Snapper*, and she's patrolling west of Lewis."

Which meant two days away from Loch Rudha. Carrick rubbed his chin.

"Clapper Bell suggested we try blasting some of the rock—"

"Not yet." Shannon shook his head in complete disapproval. "Mister, right now, I want you to take the packboat back to

Port MacFarlane. See the harbour master." He scowled to himself. "By now, half the boats on the West Coast will know about us, and be laughing their heads off. But we've still got to stick by the formalities, so put him in the picture and say we'll keep in touch."

"What did happen?" asked Carrick, still puzzled.

"Andy Shaw's still checking." Leaning his elbows on the bright brass of the compass binnacle, Shannon considered his own reflection with disgust. "We had a complete loss of hydraulics on the telemotor gear—that's all he can say so far. But I'm going to find out, Webb. I want the answer just as much as any court of inquiry will later."

.   .   .   .   .

The sun was up and the cutter already on its way by the time Carrick went below. He stripped off the scuba suit, dried himself down and changed into uniform, then had a quick cup of coffee before he went back on deck.

The packboat was waiting in the water at *Marlin*'s stern and he scrambled down into it, started the big outboard engine, and cast off. Heading away in a slow curve, he took another long look at the stranded fishery cruiser then opened the throttle and turned away.

Fifteen minutes took him back to Port MacFarlane. As he steered the packboat in past the breakwater two big drifters were going out and several boats in the harbour were in process of getting under way. He heard a few jeering shouts about the fishery cruiser as he tied the packboat to an iron-runged ladder and climbed up to the quayside.

But another voice hailed him by name as he started to walk towards the harbour master's office. It was Dan Fraser. Sleepy-eyed and dark-jowled, Fraser trotted towards him.

"The word is you've got troubles," said Fraser without preliminaries, an odd grin on his lean face.

"You can see them." Wryly, Carrick thumbed down Loch Rudha. *Marlin* was small in the distance, but the way she lay across the dog-leg channel was clearly visible.

"That?" Fraser showed a minimal sympathy. "Hard luck. But I

79

meant the troubles at Halley Bay. How much of the story is true?"

The boats preparing to stream from harbour took on a new significance. The coastal bush telegraph had been working overtime and a lot of people wanted to check on their floating bank balances.

"How much have you heard?" countered Carrick.

"That Halley Bay was raided overnight." A light gust of wind ruffled Fraser's long black hair and he brushed it back impatiently. "The word is old Francie MacPhee was left trussed like a boiling fowl and most of the lobster rafts have gone. True or false?"

"True, and about as much as we know," nodded Carrick.

Fraser gave a low, soft whistle. "That's going to upset one hell of a lot of people, Carrick."

"It doesn't exactly leave Fishery Protection laughing all over," said Carrick bleakly. "We're doing what we can."

"In between getting stuck on reefs?" asked Fraser sarcastically. He stopped and winced, putting a hand to shade his eyes against the light. "All right, that's turning the knife right now. But it was after four this morning before that damned party died and I could crawl into my bunk—then I got dragged out again for this. Right now, I've a regiment of little men with hammers working inside my skull."

"You don't marry off a brother every day," mused Carrick.

"True." Fraser managed to crinkle a grin. "And the whole whoop-up is supposed to get under way again before evening—it's my solemn duty to be in there drinking, Heaven help me." Scrubbing a hand over the dark stubble on his chin, he sighed. "Wherever Roddy and Mhari are on that wee boat, they're well clear of this lot. Still, I know what I'm doing. I'm sailing the *Razorbill* over to Horsehead Island and I'm sticking a shotgun guard on that storage pool."

"If there's anything left to guard," suggested Carrick mildly.

"That kind of crack makes us level." Fraser scowled for a moment, then brightened. "Well, today's shipment is safely over at the airstrip—and if everything's as before at the island Roddy and I could do all right out of this. A lot of people won't be able to meet their orders, and that means higher prices for those who can."

"Not if the bunch who grabbed these pens unload their stock," reminded Carrick.

"They won't, not straight away." Fraser shook his head firmly. "The market would spot it. No, they'll sell gradually, over a spell. Unless, of course, there's a small miracle and Fishery Protection catch them first."

Grinning, he loped back towards his boat leaving Carrick to walk on towards the harbour master's office.

Located in a small, very old stone building, the harbour master had a desk, a telephone, a short-wave receiver and a tyre company pin-up calendar. His name was Benson and he was a young Englishman who had served in the Royal Navy until his health failed.

"Well, I won't add to your troubles," he said laconically as Carrick finished the formal report of *Marlin*'s stranding. "Tell Captain Shannon there's nothing big due in for a couple of days, and there's plenty of room left for the fishing boats to squeeze past." A thought struck him. "Uh—two days will be long enough, I suppose?"

"If necessary, I'll carry her off on my back to make sure," agreed Carrick solemnly.

"And people say nothing ever happens up here." Benson gave a chuckle and sat back. "Not much you can do about the lobster raid now, I suppose."

"We've sent a boat round, and there are other fishery cruisers," said Carrick warily.

"But none near enough to matter." Benson thumbed at the short-wave receiver. "I had that on before you came in. The fishing boats are chattering like magpies about the Halley Bay business— and the word they're passing is there's not another fishery cruiser within two days of here."

Carrick shrugged. "We'll still do what we can."

"You'd better," said Benson dryly. "The County police can't go swimming after them, and if the fishermen catch this bunch first we might end up with an old-fashioned lynching party."

"Right now, I've a captain who'd happily supply the rope," mused Carrick.

"Who'd blame him?" agreed Benson. "But I mean it, Carrick. That old watchman who was clobbered has been twittering on the 'phone to various people. Like to guess the possible value of lobsters taken?" He smiled at Carrick's silence. "At least 20,000 pounds."

Carrick whistled sadly.

"It could be more," warned Benson. "The average West Highland lobster weigh around a couple of pounds, right? And the skippers around here reckon on getting a pound per pound weight, quayside prices—so that's only talking in terms of ten thousand lobsters. Halley Bay was stocking three or four times more than that."

"Any more bad news for me?" queried Carrick.

"Not right now." Benson grinned sympathetically. "You people are going to have transport problems while this is going on. Would a car be any help?"

"It might." Carrick wasn't sure what was on his mind. "The police will help out, I suppose. Or we can order a Department vehicle over from the mainland."

"You can use mine, if you like." Benson opened a desk drawer, pulled out a set of car keys, and tossed them over. "The old Ford laying outside—I only need it at weekends. Consider it yours for now, and drop the keys back in here when you're finished."

Carrick thanked him and left. The Ford, a dusty well-used Cortina station wagon, was parked at the side of the hut as Benson had said, and he ran an eye over it briefly. Whether they'd need it or not would depend on Shannon's plans, but the offer had been friendly.

Jingling the keys in his pocket, he turned away and collided almost head-on with Jimsy MacLean at the corner of the hut.

"Watch where you're damned well going," snarled the retired sea-captain, a pent-up fury behind the words. MacLean's face was tired and grey in the morning light, as if he'd had little sleep. Even the slacks and old tweed jacket he was wearing seemed to hang limp on his thin frame. But as he recognised Carrick, he gave

82

a curt nod. "I'm looking for Dan Fraser. Any idea why his boat is out?"

"He's gone over to Horsehead Island—he wants to check his storage pool." Carrick saw the blank lack of understanding on MacLean's face, and added, "The rafts at Halley Bay were raided last night."

"I heard." MacLean dismissed the fact and ran an almost agitated hand along the thong which held his black eye-patch in place. "Damn the man. When will he be back?"

"He didn't say." Carrick shook his head.

MacLean swore bitterly under his breath and stood chewing his lip for a moment.

"Something wrong?" asked Carrick.

"No. No, I—there was just something I had to see him about." MacLean looked past him towards the harbour as if willing the *Razorbill* to appear again. "It can wait."

Carrick wondered. "If you've had another visitor like that fire-bomb maniac—"

"I said there was nothing wrong," snapped MacLean, cutting him short. Then he stopped, sighed, and forced a friendlier manner. "It was just a detail left over from the wedding, but a fairly urgent one—that's all."

"The wedding went well," said Carrick. "They make a nice couple."

"Yes." MacLean nodded absently. "Carrick, if you see Dan Fraser first—"

"I'll tell him." Carrick agreed amiably, moving aside to let the older man pass. He did it awkwardly, they brushed together again and he murmured an apology. Grunting rudely, MacLean strode off, heading back towards the village.

Carrick watched him go. The second near-collision had been deliberate. It had been enough to confirm what his eyes had suspected and what Captain Shannon had claimed earlier . . . Jimsy MacLean was again carrying a gun in his hip pocket.

But there was something else. MacLean and Shannon were allegedly long and close friends. *Marlin* was stranded down the channel in clear view, anyone in Port MacFarlane who wasn't either blind or deaf had to know about it—yet MacLean hadn't thought it worth a mention, sympathetic or otherwise.

Even from a man with MacLean's assorted problems that was in the category of downright odd.

. . . . .

It was close on nine a.m. when Carrick arrived back aboard *Marlin*. The fishery cruiser's pumps were still throbbing as he left the packboat and climbed on deck, but the flow of water was down to little more than a trickle and there was a new optimism aboard. Even the usually truculent Pettigrew had something close to a smile on his sour, lined face.

"We're pretty well patched up for'ard," he told Carrick as they met near the bridge companionway. "If the Old Man gets us off without bending anything more we can head back for repairs without too much worry."

"It'll be a dockyard job," mused Carrick. "From what I saw, maybe a month ashore."

Pettigrew's smile faded. Then he shrugged.

"I'll worry about that if it happens," he said briefly, and disappeared below again.

Captain Shannon was on the bridge with a mug of coffee and Andy Shaw, the chief engineer, for company. But there were no smiles evident on either of their faces. Shannon nodded briefly at Carrick's report then turned to Shaw.

"Tell him," he said curtly.

"Aye, and I'll keep it short." Shaw, a lanky man in the inevitably oil-stained overalls of his profession, wrinkled his grimy face in distaste. "But that doesn't make it any better."

"Well?" Carrick waited.

"I was told to find out why the steering went all to hell," said Shaw with a sideways glance at Shannon. "Now you know how the telemotor gear works, Webb—hydraulics, fluid under pressure. Turn the steering wheel and it's like power assistance on a car. The piped fluid actuates the rudder as required—"

"You said you'd keep it short," said Shannon bleakly.

"I am," said Shaw stubbornly. "But the basics matter, Captain—if any o' you deck people are to understand anyway." He turned back to Carrick. "In harbour, once the engines have stopped, there's no pressure in the system—none that matters anyway. That only happens when you start the engines again, right?"

Carrick nodded, still puzzled.

"Fine." Shaw looked relieved. "Because the steering failed due to a complete dam' lack of hydraulic pressure. And I found out why when I followed these pipes along below deck. There was a dam' great pool of oil near the lamp-room aft—and a hole that could only have been made with a hand-drill in the pipe above."

"He means it was sabotage, mister," said Shannon in a harsh voice. He stopped, his face tightening. Another fishing boat was heading out of the loch, going past *Marlin*'s stern at a slow crawl. The shouts and jeers from her crew showed their delight at the fishery crusier's temporary disgrace. "Someone—either in this crew or who got aboard—didn't want us to leave Loch Rudha."

It had taken a moment or two to sink home. But there was still one part which didn't seem to make sense to Carrick.

"Andy, we were using the rudder constantly coming out of harbour—and coming down the loch." He still had the rest of it clear in his memory. "The first hint we had was when the helmsman said she was handling sluggishly. But even then—"

"Why didn't it fail straight off?" Shaw nodded his understanding. Reaching into an overall pocket, he brought out a crumpled, dirty piece of broad white insulating tape. "There's your answer. The basket who did this didn't want us to spot the fluid leak in harbour, where it would have been easy enough to fix. So he bandaged round the hole he'd made, just enough to hold the initial pressure."

"Then the fluid started leaking, response became sluggish—and total failure." Shannon drew a deep breath. "That's it, mister. He left us with a few minutes' sailing time in one of the worst damned channels on this whole coast."

Carrick felt a shiver run down his back. Even stranded as they were, they'd been lucky. On another reef, in different weather or a dozen other circumstances the result could have been disaster with *Marlin* a sunken wreck and perhaps even a steel tomb for some of her crew.

"How many know, sir?" he asked quietly.

"The three of us, plus Clapper Bell. He helped Andy find the trouble."

The bridge intercom buzzed. Swearing softly, Shannon strode over, answered it, then gave a curt order to the man at the other end to call back. Hanging up, he faced them again.

"Three of us and Bell. I want it kept that way for now, mister."

"Where's the benefit?" asked Andy Shaw, puzzled. "The character who did this is bound to know we've found that hole by now."

"Because I want to keep him guessing any way I can," said Shannon softly. "Guessing and worried. If it was one of the crew, that's one thing. But the other possibility—think of that a moment, both of you. The raid on Halley Bay, for a start."

"But what the hell—" began Shaw, then fell silent.

"Halley Bay," repeated Shannon in the same grimly practical voice. "All right, tell a city man that someone rustled a damned herd of lobsters and he might think it funny. But tell him the local bank was done for 30,000 pounds and he'll squeal loud enough."

Carrick frowned. "They saying 20,000 pounds ashore, sir."

"And I'm saying thirty—minimum. Young Wills radioed in from the bay." Shannon pursed his lips for an instant. "No trace of the rafts or pens that have gone, no trace of how it was done. But someone did a lot of careful planning round the MacLean wedding night."

Then *Marlin* had come sailing in, and had to be dealt with. That had taken nerve and know-how, they all knew. But perhaps not too much risk once the intruder was aboard. The lamp-room aft was a seldom visited area when they were in harbour.

"But when?" Carrick asked the question aloud without really meaning to speak.

"A good point, mister," nodded Shannon. He drew a deep breath. "Suppose it was two nights ago? The same night we had to fish a dead man out of the harbour?"

Shannon had been thinking ahead of him, not for the first time. But the next stage in that particular direction would have to come from the autopsy report on Christie.

A little later, Andy Shaw headed back for the engine room. That gave Carrick the chance he'd wanted and he told Shannon about Jimsy MacLean's behaviour—and the gun he was carrying.

"It'll have to wait, mister," said Shannon with a slow headshake. "We've got our own priorities now." Reaching into his inside pocket, he brought out a folded slip of paper and handed it over. "Better read that."

Carrick unfolded the radio room message flimsy. It was a signal from Department, sent in plain language, addressed personally to Shannon.

"CONTINUE ADVISE SHIP STATUS, ON REFLOAT, BERTH AT PORT MACFARLANE PENDING DAMAGE SURVEY. ON COMPLETION REPORT IN PERSON, FLOTILLA HQ LEITH."

He handed it back with a grimace. "They can't blame you—particularly now."

"They can ask why our security wasn't better, for a start." Shannon put the slip of paper away. "Well, that's my worry, mister. But take another trip ashore. Ask the harbour master for a list of every boat that has visited Port MacFarlane over the last couple of weeks. There's an outside chance it might help—and right now, outside chances are all we've got."

．　　　．　　　．　　　．　　　．

High water would be at four minutes before three p.m., still hours away, but there was plenty to do in the interval. The damage to the bow sufficiently patched, *Marlin's* crew turned to lightening ship for'ard in every possible way. The engine room helped by trimming her diesel tanks so that the bulk of the fuel was pumped from the midship tanks to the aft tanks. At the same time, Andy Shaw finished repairs on the telemotor gear and began putting it through a rigorous series of tests.

Carrick did his share. But he was with Clapper Bell in the scuba storeroom aft when two short klaxon horn blasts and a low murmur of engines signalled still another craft going down the loch towards the sea.

Stubbing the cigarette he'd been smoking, Clapper Bell ambled over to the storeroom door then beckoned Carrick.

Long and low, her bow wave little more than a ripple, the
San Helena was easing past their stern. One of the motor yacht's
crew was meticulously coiling the bow mooring line, another
worked on the speedboat she carried aft, and Dirk Peters was at
the wheel on her cockpit bridge with Frank Farrell beside him,
both eyeing the fishery cruiser closely as they passed.

Seeing Carrick, they waved a greeting.

"Hard luck," called Peters. "Anything we can do?"

"No, you might get your paintwork dirty," answered Carrick.

Peters grinned. They saw him move the hand throttles forward
as the *San Helena* got clear. Her engines barked, a momentary
cloud of oily blue exhaust showed at her stern, then she began
gathering speed and headed down Loch Rudha in a broad white
wake.

CHAPTER FIVE

Marlin's cutter radioed in another report half an hour later. Jumbo Wills and his boat's crew were continuing their search along the coastline, but still without success. A total silence from the County police indicated that things weren't any better on the landward side.

It was as if the lobster rafts and the men who had taken them had never existed—and the only bright spot was a signal from Department which said that the Navy had agreed to alert any air patrols passing over the area and would back this up later if necessary with a spotter helicopter.

The fishery cruiser's launch had begun acting as a ferry service between the reef and Port MacFarlane. As soon as he was clear of more immediate tasks, Webb Carrick used it for a trip back to harbour and went straight to the harbour master's office. Benson was still there and listened sympathetically to Captain Shannon's request for a list of boats.

"No problem there," he assured Carrick. "How soon do you need this list?"

"Whenever you've got the time."

"All right." Benson flicked through the pages of his day-ledger and nodded. "Give me an hour or so. And you can tell him we'll have a few vacant berths by this afternoon. Jimsy MacLean says he's cancelling the rest of the wedding celebrations, so some of our visitors will be heading back to work."

"He's cancelling?" Carrick raised a surprised eyebrow, but remembered MacLean's mood when he'd seen him. "Did he give any reason?"

"Not to me," shrugged the harbour master. "But a lot of the

89

locals are feeling sick about what happened at Halley Bay There's that—or maybe he just wants to save money."

Carrick thanked him, promised to come back for the list, and left. Outside, he paused for a moment then searched for the car keys in his pocket and went over to Benson's station wagon. Unlocking it, he got behind the wheel then hesitated and finally made up his mind. Starting the car, he drove out of the harbour and headed up towards the house on the hill.

When he reached Ard-Tulach, he saw Tara Grant's little two-seater parked near the front door. The smashed front window of the house had been boarded up.

Climbing the steps, he rang the bell and waited. The housekeeper opened the door after a few moments and greeted him nervously, fading back with relief as Tara Grant appeared.

"I didn't expect to see you for a spell." Tara, in a sweater and jeans, her feet in sandals, smiled and gestured up towards the turret window. "I've been using Jimsy MacLean's telescope, watching what's been going on down the loch. How did it happen?"

"A steering failure," he said briefly. "But things could be worse. There's not too much damage and with a little luck we'll get off again with the tide."

"Good." She seemed pleased, then frowned apologetically. "I must have been asleep when it happened. The first thing I knew this morning was the telephone ringing—I think Jimsy MacLean must have answered it. Then I heard him going out and driving away. Probably he wanted to see for himself. But—well, I went straight back to sleep again."

"You had a late night," said Carrick mildly.

"Yes." Her blue-grey eyes met and held his for a moment. "Yes, I had. A rather special night." Then she gave a quick, small gesture. "Now—things just seem chaotic all round. I heard about the Halley Bay business."

He nodded. "No more trouble here?"

"Nothing I know about—and if you're looking for Jimsy MacLean, he went out again about fifteen minutes ago." She shook her head pensively. "But he's more on edge than ever—Effie says she has never seen him so bad."

"I know what Effie means—I saw him earlier," said Carrick dryly. "Why has he cancelled the rest of the wedding feast?"

"All I got were some growls about it being no time for festivities," grimaced Tara. "Then he said he was driving over to Halley Bay to see things for himself. If you want him badly enough, that's where you'll find him."

Surprised, Carrick pursed his lips for a moment. "What's he driving?"

"A blue Volkswagen." She tucked her thumbs into the waistband of her jeans. "Any sense in asking if you'd like to wait here?"

"I'd like, but I can't," he said sadly. "I've a captain who wouldn't appreciate it. But once we've got *Marlin* back in harbour things will be different."

She nodded. "I'll settle for that, as long as the atmosphere up here doesn't get worse."

Grinning, Carrick left her and went back to the station wagon. She was still standing in the doorway as he drove off.

. . . . . .

He stopped briefly at the harbour to tell the rating in charge of the launch that he'd be gone for a spell then turned the station wagon on the road for Halley Bay.

It was narrow, winding, climbing road that soon became single-track with occasional passing places as it took a wide, snaking curve through the hills. Sheep were grazing on the unfenced verges and once he saw a young roe deer scamper away. There were clouds overhead, all scudding across the sky before a gathering wind, and he had a feeling the next weather forecast they received on *Marlin* wouldn't be particularly welcome.

The road wound on. A car and a couple of rattling farm trucks passed him, heading in for Port MacFarlane, but that was all apart from the occasional roadside sign pointing towards a track with a tiny cottage or farmhouse somewhere at its end. Then, surprisingly, he reached a cross-roads junction. The main trunk road for Tobermory, the island's only real town, went off to the left. The road ahead led towards Fionnphort and the ferry crossing to Iona but to the right the signpost said Halley Bay.

Carrick turned and accelerated. It was an even narrower road this time, little more than a track—and it climbed viciously to the top of a heather-clad ridge before giving him a glimpse of the sea and plunging down again.

Then, still descending with the Ford in low gear, he saw Halley Bay ahead—and at the same time spotted a blue Volkswagen drawn in beside some rocks below, well off the road. Slowing, Carrick lost it for a moment as a fold of ground intervened, glimpsed the roof again, and had a third view a moment later which showed him there was someone aboard it.

Puzzled, he brought the borrowed station wagon down to a crawl then saw his chance and swung the wheel, bumping the car in tyre-punishing fashion onto a patch of rough but comparatively level ground littered with small boulders. When he stopped, he was out of sight of the road and at least as well sheltered as the Volkswagen below.

Switching off, Carrick climbed out. A ridge of gorse and rock blocked his view of the other car and he clambered up the slope, still not completely certain why he was doing things that way but keeping behind the cover of the gorse as he reached the top.

He was looking down on the Volkswagen and it was Jimsy MacLean who was aboard it, smoking a cigarette and watching the bay below.

A solitary police car was parked beside the huts and the only boat was the watchman's work-launch, drawn up on the sand at the water's edge. Some of the lobster pens were still moored in position but there were gaps—and two of the big wooden rafts had drifted ashore then been stranded by the tide.

Carrick took a half-step forward then hesitated and stayed where he was. Whatever MacLean's reason for wanting to stay hidden, barging down and challenging him wouldn't help.

Crouching down, he waited while insects buzzed and crawled through the gorse around him. The Volkswagen's window wound down briefly and a cigarette end was tossed out. The minutes dragged past and Carrick grew stiff and weary. He changed his position again then, down at the huts, figures appeared. Two uniformed policemen and a third figure in civilian clothes boarded the police car.

The police car started up, swung away from the huts, and began travelling up the road from the bay. In a couple of minutes it purred past, climbing towards the main road. Seconds later, Jimsy MacLean's car growled to life, reversed cautiously out of its hiding place, then drove down towards the huts.

It stopped there and MacLean climbed out. One brief glance around, and he headed for the nearest hut and went in.

Carrick shrugged to himself, lit a cigarette, and waited again. The cigarette was a mashed-out stub beside him and forgotten when MacLean at last reappeared, the smaller figure of Francie MacPhee, the watchman, beside him.

They had a last, brief conversation beside the car then MacPhee turned on his heel and went back. As he disappeared, Jimsy MacLean climbed slowly into the Volkswagen but another full minute elapsed before the blue car began moving up the road.

With a wry feeling that he'd become part of a bizarre follow-my-leader game, Carrick let the Volkswagen drive past then returned to the station wagon. Backing it out, he drove towards the huts.

When he stopped and climbed out he was immediately conscious he was being watched. But he stayed where he was for a moment, looking out at the bay again, noting the irregular gaps in the pattern of the remaining rafts and pens.

"Aye, they knew what they were after," grumbled a voice behind him.

He turned and nodded. Francie MacPhee was standing in the doorway of the smaller hut. The old man had a slash of white bandage wound round his head like an economy-size turban and his weatherbeaten face had a frown on it just one shade short of a scowl.

"How about you?" asked Carrick.

MacPhee shrugged. "I've taken a wee thump on the head afore now. But they tied me up damned tight." His eyes swept Carrick's uniform briefly. "You're the Fishery Protection mannie who was here yesterday."

"That's right." Carrick strolled easily towards him. "That's when you said you could supply all the protection needed around here."

"So I was wrong." MacPhee sniffed indignantly. "But thumpin' you on the head from behind isn't my idea of a fair fight."

"Complain to the referee next time," suggested Carrick sardonically. "How many were there in the raid?"

"Hell, I don't know," protested MacPhee. "There was a noise outside the hut in the middle o' the night, I went out to have a look, an'—" he smacked a fist against his palm with a grimace. "Next thing I knew, I was roped up an' had a sack over my head. On top o' that, they'd shoved me under my bed. I didn't have much o' a view believe me."

"But you could still hear," reminded Carrick. "How about voices?"

"None I knew."

"Or when they towed the pens away?"

MacPhee shrugged. "Just a boat engine, maybe two engines— fishin' boat size. That's all, like I told the fellow from your outfit who was here already. Can't remember his name, but you should have a collar round his neck in case he gets lost."

"Second Officer Wills," nodded Carrick, poker-faced. He thumbed out towards the remaining rafts. "How many were taken?"

"Five." MacPhee scratched his chest through his overalls and scowled.

"The easiest to tow and the most valuable?" queried Carrick. "As if they knew exactly which to take?"

MacPhee nodded dourly.

"How about the Frasers' raft?"

"On the beach over there," grunted MacPhee, thumbing past him. "It's one o' the couple that were cut loose but left, maybe so they could tow the others out. The thing got pretty bashed up when it grounded. They can write it off, that's for sure—an' what was in it."

"Was that why Jimsy MacLean came over?" asked Carrick softly.

"Captain MacLean?" The man's wrinkled face showed an immediate caution. "Who says he's been here?"

"I saw him leaving," said Carrick wearily. "Why did he come?"

"Just to hear what had happened," shrugged MacPhee.

"Nothing else?"

"Like what?" grunted the watchman stubbornly. "If there was, it would be my business, right?"

"Wrong." Unhurriedly, Carrick took him by the front of the overalls and brought him a couple of inches nearer. "MacPhee, until this mess is sorted out you're going to be asked a lot of questions. So get used to it, understand?"

Licking his lips, MacPhee nodded. Carrick let him go.

"Well?"

"It wasn't anythin' much, Chief." The man's face twitched in a slightly frightened, gap-toothed grin. "He—well, he said there were one or two folk around who might have it in for the Frasers, an' that I wouldn't do myself any good if I made any hints in that direction."

MacPhee attempted a leer. "Och, I told him it was a daft notion anyway. For a start, young Roddy would have better things to do on his weddin' night, eh?"

"That was all?"

MacPhee nodded. He was lying, Carrick was sure of it. There were tiny beads of perspiration gathering on the man's forehead and his eyes kept avoiding a direct meeting. But whatever MacLean had come for, whatever he'd said, the truth would have to be levered out of MacPhee the hard way—and for the moment, at least, the lever was missing.

"I'll be back," said Carrick shortly. "Have a think about things, MacPhee. You're in the kind of spot where it doesn't help to be awkward."

"Hell, maybe this bang on the head has left things a wee bit mixed, Chief." MacPhee moistened his lips. "But if I remember anythin', I'll let you know, an' straight away. That's a promise."

Carrick left him and went back to the station wagon. Driving away, he saw the man through the rear-view mirror. There was a

95

new expression on Francie MacPhee's face, a mixture of fear and worry—as if MacPhee very much had something to think about.

.   .   .   .   .

A few drops of rain showed on the windscreen on the journey back, but the sun was shining again when Carrick reached Port MacFarlane. Before he returned to the harbour, he made a detour past Ard-Tulach. Jimsy MacLean's blue Volkswagen was lying in the driveway beside Tara's two-seater, but there was no other sign of life.

He left the station wagon in its parking place at the harbour, collected the list of boats lying ready for him at the harbour master's office, and began walking along the quay to where *Marlin*'s launch was in again, loading some stores. Then, just beyond it, he saw the *Razorbill* was also back in, her crew stacking empty lobsters boxes from the quay to her fishhold.

Carrick went over. A fisherman hosing down the decks saw him, abandoned the hose for a moment, and ambled to the wheelhouse. Almost immediately, Dan Fraser emerged and gave him a grin and a wave before scrambling up to the quay to join him.

"How were things at Horsehead Island?" asked Carrick.

"Fine—untouched by human hand, thank the Lord," said Fraser cheerfully, then gave a slight grimace. "Our pen at Halley Bay's pretty much of a write-off, but at that we're still damned lucky."

"Luckier than most," agreed Carrick. He thumbed past Fraser to the continuing flow of lobster boxes being loaded aboard the drifter. "Looks like you're not wasting time either."

"That's right." Fraser was unabashed. "I'm leaving one man on guard on Horsehead Island, just in case. But I'm planning to make a couple of runs with stock—the market will grab them."

"Which may not make you popular," mused Carrick.

"I'll worry about that when it happens." The tall, thin fisherman combed a hand through his long hair and chuckled. "You watch what happens, Carrick—I won't be the only one who grabs this kind of chance by the short and curlies."

Carrick nodded. Fishing was business, messy, muscle-racking, often dangerous business—whatever the romantics might think, however many dreams there were of red sails in the sunset or any of the rest, it came down to earning a living. With the size of profit achieved by the fishermen small enough in proportion to the risks they ran and the percentages achieved by the middlemen ashore.

"Just don't push your luck," he said quietly.

"Me?" Fraser winked. "I know what I'm doing. But I've got to go up and see Jimsy MacLean first—he's been leaving messages all round saying he wants me for something."

"I know he cancelled the rest of the wedding jamboree," Carrick told him. "He says this is the wrong time."

Fraser blinked. "I'd have put it the other way round, that there are a few characters who could use a drink after this lot." He glanced at his wrist-watch. "I'd better get it over with, anyway. Time's going to be money for the next couple of days, and I've still to fix some extra flights with the air-freight people."

"You'll soon be in the Farrell class," said Carrick dryly.

"Farrell?" Fraser laughed with an ironic edge. "I'd never make a desk-bound mini-tycoon, Carrick. I might have a go at his pal's game if I had the chance—loafing around in a boat like the *San Helena* with a few crates of liquor and all mod con. Except I'd crew her with dolly-birds."

"Let me know if it happens," agreed Carrick, fighting down a smile. "I might sign on for a trip."

"You'd get in the queue, friend, like everyone else." Fraser gave him a mock salute and ambled off towards the village.

Marlin's launch was ready to leave, the coxswain waiting patiently at the helm. Carrick stood for a moment longer, watching Fraser, then went back along the quay and climbed aboard.

．　　　．　　　．　　　．　　　．

The noon shipping forecast broadcast by the B.B.C. was positive and gloomy for the Hebridean area. Heavy cloud and rain were due from the north-west, with strengthening winds up to Force Six and rising. But Captain Shannon seemed happy at the prospect. Inside Loch Rudha, the result might mean an inch or two more water under *Marlin's* hull at high tide—an inch or two that might make all the difference to the stranded fishery cruiser.

He was studying a readiness report with Pettigrew in the chart-room when Carrick arrived but finished that quickly and sent the junior second mate on his way. Taking the harbour master's list, he listened silently while Carrick brought him up to date with the rest then shrugged.

"It all still has to wait, mister." He let a pencil roll down the chart table, watching the angled surface pensively. *Marlin* was canted about ten degrees to port, which told its own story of how the combination of reef and tide below still held her. "I'd another signal from Department. This damage surveyor they're sending up won't reach us till tomorrow—he'll bring what they've dug out about the way Jimsy MacLean salvaged that damned oil tanker. Until then, we're wasting our time."

"How about the rest of it, sir?" queried Carrick. "Any word from the County police?"

"Nothing fresh on Halley Bay, not a chirp about the Christie post-mortem result." Shannon swore softly into his beard. "We're having a visitor later—a Detective Inspector Jason they've sent over from Oban to handle their side of things. I told them to have him arrive after high water—if they know when that is—otherwise he'd be a damned nuisance to have around."

Carrick left him and went below. With the main engine still silent, even the generator's purring note seemed strangely subdued while the occasional rasping groan as *Marlin*'s hull shifted slightly against the reef had an eerie, unreal quality as if the fishery cruiser was protesting at the indignity of it all.

His cabin had been tidied by the wardroom steward. Somehow, against all the rest, it seemed smaller than ever. A raucous eruption of seagulls outside the porthole as the galley slops were emptied over the side kept him amused for a moment or two, then he gave up.

Waiting was something he didn't enjoy. But nothing could hurry the tide.

· · · · ·

The cutter returned from its unsuccessful search patrol at 13.40 hours, the crew hungry and cursing as they helped in the task of having the boat brought aboard again. When he reached the wardroom, Jumbo Wills flopped into a chair and gestured miserably.

"A complete ruddy waste of time, that's all it was," he complained. "If anyone wants, I can now give a lecture on just about every bay and inlet on this side of Mull. But the biggest thing we found was a dead sheep—did the Old Man really expect these damned lobster rafts were going to be left tied up round a corner somewhere?"

"You were showing the flag," soothed Carrick. "Fishery Protection in action—independent command."

Scowling, Jumbo Wills told him exactly what Fishery Protection could do with his particular sample of independent command. But he brightened as the wardroom steward brought him a meal.

"What's been happening here anyway?" he asked, as he began eating. "Are we all set to go yet?"

"Any time," agreed Carrick, wooden-faced. "But the Old Man thought we'd better wait till you got back. He might need your advice."

Wills half-choked on a mouthful of beef stew.

"And up yours too," he said bleakly. "What's for pudding?"

High Water was due at 15.03 hours and its coming was signalled minute by minute as the fishery cruiser's list gradually decreased, accompanied by an occasional creak and groan along her hull.

Fifteen minutes before high water Captain Shannon ordered hands to stations and the diesels fired up. The familiar vibration began underfoot, a light blue haze of exhaust began throbbing from the fishery cruiser's funnel, and while Pettigrew's damage control party moved forward the bridge loud-hailer rasped a brusque warning to a couple of fishing boats which had appeared as interested spectators. A new flag hoist went up, repeating the "stay clear" warning to any others who arrived.

On the bridge, Shannon glanced at the roll pendulum, now almost exactly on the perpendicular, then at the ticking seconds hand of the chronometer dial.

"Now, I think, mister," he said softly, standing with his nose almost pressed against the glass of the main window, his hands clasped behind his back. "Engine room stand by."

"Sir." Carrick repeated the order on the bridge intercom 'phone. From the other end, he heard Andy Shaw mutter to himself.

"Both slow astern—gently." Shannon's hands tightened slightly as Carrick repeated the order and the diesels began to change in note. "Increase revolutions."

A new shudder ran through *Marlin* as her twin screws began to bite. Gradually, as the power built up, the shudder increased and the sea water at her stern began to boil to a white fury.

"Webb—" Andy Shaw's voice came like an anxious cackle over the intercom line "—better tell him he's getting damn near the limit."

Carrick ignored him. Shannon's hands were clenched knuckle-white, the whole ship was visibly shaking as she fought to break free—but she still wasn't moving.

"Maximum revolutions," ordered Shannon greyly, one eye on the chronometer's remorseless timekeeping. "Emergency full astern, mister."

"Emergency full," repeated Carrick.

The shudder grew worse as four thousand horsepower poured and moaned through the twin shafts below. The tinkle of breaking glass reached them, and heavier crashes. Then, suddenly, Shannon gave a sigh and shook his head.

"No use, mister. She'll shake herself to death first. Stop engines. Resume standby routing—see me in my cabin."

His small, thickset figure had vanished from the bridge long before the engines had finished dying.

Five minutes later, the pumps at work again to cope with a new leakage of water that had started up near the bow, Carrick knocked on the day-cabin door and went in.

Shannon was seated at his desk, grimly completing a new personal log-entry. He wrote on for a moment then slapped the log-book shut and looked up.

"I've a choice now, mister," he said bluntly. "I can wait for a tug to haul us off—nothing around here could be of much help.

Or I can listen again to those noises you made earlier about explosives."

"Sir." Carrick nodded slowly. "It was Clapper Bell's notion—but it might work. There's one main spur of rock that has us pretty much like it was a fish-hook. If we used a small charge, just small enough to get rid of it—" he stopped, waiting.

"You know what that could do to our hull?" rasped Shannon. "It could slice us like a tin-opener."

"I know what a tug could do the other way," said Carrick stubbornly. "Two wire hawsers on our stern and heave away—let's get this cork out of the bottle."

Shannon winced and frowned pensively for a moment. It was easy to guess what he was thinking. In any kind of underwater blasting the shock waves could be tricky. One charge, exactly placed could do its job and cause hardly any outside effect. But another, with just a slight mistake, could cause as much damage as a runaway steam hammer.

"We'd use a series of charges, sir," suggested Carrick. "Blasting gelatine, sequence detonation—five-second intervals."

Sequence charges, with a regular time interval between each blast, would keep the shock waves to a minimum. But with explosives there was always a gamble—which would be Shannon's gamble, whatever happened.

For a few moments more Shannon said nothing, his stubby fingers tapping the desk.

"Go ahead, mister," he said suddenly. "If it works, we'll have another try at getting off when next high water comes round. After that, it's a tug job." He stopped Carrick as he turned to go. "But don't start diving until this County detective has been aboard. I'll want you around for that."

The pumps were still spurting as Carrick went aft. For once, Clapper Bell wasn't in the scuba storeroom but he located the bo'sun in another of his favourite hideaways, the galley.

Beckoning Bell out, ignoring the way the cook's apron had swept across a pack of cards, Carrick waited at the ship's rail until the Glasgow-Irishman arrived.

"The Old Man says we can have a go with explosives," he said and saw Bell beam. "We'll have to make it a delayed action harness job, Clapper—minimum charges, anchored down."

"I could have bet on it." Bell nodded happily. "I've got most o' what we'll need ready. How soon do we go down?"

Carrick frowned. A launch was coming out from the harbour towards them, one passenger aboard. The County police didn't seem to believe in wasting time.

"Half an hour," he decided. "Have everything rigged. But minimum charges, Clapper—remember that."

"They'll be as gentle as an angel's kiss," promised Bell, and went off jauntily.

.   .   .   .   .   .

Detective Inspector Peter Jason came aboard *Marlin* in the kind of awkward scramble which showed he didn't know much about ships and the sea. He was met by Captain Shannon, they disappeared into the day-cabin together, and several minutes passed before Carrick was summoned by a messenger.

When he went in, the policeman was sitting back in a chair with a glass of whisky in one hand. Shannon also had a drink and gestured towards a third glass and the waiting bottle.

"Help yourself, mister," he instructed as he finished the introductions. "You may need it."

Carrick poured a drink, noting that Jason hadn't rated the single-malt stock which *Marlin*'s commander kept for guests who mattered. Then he sipped his glass and waited, glancing at Jason. The detective inspector was a slim, sparse man with dark hair, brown eyes and a face that might have looked at home on a Wanted poster. He wore a threadbare tweed suit with leather patches at the elbows and when he spoke his voice had a clipped, almost military accent.

"It seems the police have problems too," said Shannon dryly, leading off. "One of them is the Christie post mortem, mister."

"Because of circumstance and a pathologist who, for our sins, is maybe brighter than most," said Jason patiently, a man repeating what he'd already gone through once. He turned to Carrick. "We're dealing with a drunken fisherman who gets himself involved in a couple of fights. Then he—well, your people fish him out of the harbour. The autopsy report establishes he was alive when he went in. But there's a rider added—that the odds were he was unconscious at the time."

"We've people who heard him shout for help," reminded Carrick, stifling his surprise. "At least two of them our own men."

"They heard somebody shout once," corrected Jason curtly. He rubbed a hand along his chin unhappily. "But our pathologist says —hell, don't ask me for it in words you or I can understand. He gabbles on about chloride of the blood, lung contents and the rest. Then about head injuries—and don't tell me he was bashed with a bottle. I know that."

"So it could have been murder," grunted Shannon.

The policeman nodded. "Or at least I've got to treat it that way. Then, if we tie in the possibility that your steering gear was sabotaged the same night and add on what happened at Halley Bay—" he sucked his teeth noisily and shrugged "—well, there's a pattern all right."

Shannon took a swallow of whisky from his glass and raised an eyebrow in Carrick's direction.

"We were halfway towards that ourselves," said Carrick slowly. "If Christie was on the quayside and saw a stranger sneaking aboard *Marlin*—"

"Sneaking aboard or leaving," nodded Jason. "He saw too much, somebody got scared—and got rid of him. Shove him over the edge, wait for the splash, fake a shout for help, then get the hell out of it, fast." Finishing his drink at a gulp, he got to his feet. "My notion about all this isn't going to be popular—but right now I'd give a lot to lay my hands on young Roddy Fraser."

"I already told you he was with us most of that evening," said Shannon grimly. "And he was back aboard their boat before the alarm went up about Christie." He saw the expression on Jason's face and scowled. "All right, then he claims he was—and he can probably produce a boatload of witnesses."

"Like his brother. I've talked to Dan Fraser." The detective nodded calmly. "Captain, once you get your ship out of her present—ah—predicament I imagine you'll really get down to chasing those lobster rustlers. Don't be too surprised if you find a Fraser among them."

"I'd like one good reason," murmured Carrick, watching Shannon purpling.

"One?" Jason nodded. "I checked their bank situation. They've been making money all right, quite a lot of money at the lobster game. Enough to keep up the payments on that boat." He walked towards the cabin door then half-turned to face them. "But not enough to pay for a second boat they happen to have ordered. I'll ah—keep in touch, Captain."

He went out. As the cabin door closed again Shannon swore vitriolically.

"Once you get your ship out of her present predicament—" he thumped the nearest bulkhead with his fist, "mister, I like to think of myself as reasonably placid by nature. But if that long, miserable refugee from handing out parking tickets comes aboard like that again I bloody well won't answer for the consequences."

"But what he said might make sense," said Carrick reluctantly.

"That makes it worse," flared Shannon. "God help us if I'd let him get a sniff of Jimsy MacLean's troubles." His irritation continued to grow. "Why the hell are you standing around anyway, mister? You've got a job to do, haven't you?"

Captain James Shannon's definition of "placid" came from a dictionary all his own.

.   .   .   .   .

Carrick and Clapper Bell swam down to the reef again half an hour later and by then the weather forecast was becoming justified. A grey drizzle of rain came from the heavily clouded sky, the wind was rising steadily, and a heavy, greasy swell had begun coming up the loch.

Under the surface, conditions had also changed. In the shallow depth at which they were working unseen eddies and current plucked and pulled at their bodies while they began their task in the shimmering light.

A rubberised haversack clipped to the front of each man's weight belt held all he needed. The main item was the harness of submarine blasting gelignite, seven small cup-shaped charges in individual canvas pouches linked together by light rope. Clapper Bell's handiwork had them neatly wired in series, the detonators with their vital chemical delay elements doubly checked before they'd gone down.

It took time to examine the spur again then scrape its base clear of weed. More time to place the charges and tape them firmly in position using the grain of the rock for maximum effect yet making sure the results would still be minimal in terms of the shockwave which would reach out towards *Marlin*'s hull.

But at last it was done. They surfaced and came back aboard.

A small audience had gathered on the foredeck, Captain Shannon among them, and watched silently as Clapper Bell carefully connected the free ends of the firing wires to the exploder box.

Carrick had the contact key. Silently, he handed the key to the bo'sun who slotted it in place and glanced round at Shannon.

Shannon nodded and the key turned. Down below, the fuse-heads of all seven detonators were ignited by the half-amp current then the delay elements took over.

The first charge was felt like a low hammer-blow aboard the fishery cruiser while a small eruption of water drenched over her rail. Carrick waited tight-lipped as the explosions followed at their five-second intervals.

The timing was vital to reduce the underwater shock resonance waves. But the cup-shape of the charges mattered too—for what explosives men called the Munroe effect, a greater penetration concentration than if the gelignite had been slapped in place as a solid charge.

The seventh hammer-blow and accompanying spout of water came at last. A few small, dead fish were floating on the swell as Carrick and Bell went down again.

The rock spur had been shattered neatly across its base. Bubbles pluming from their outlet valves, they solemnly shook hands then Bell grabbed one of the smaller chunks of broken rock as a souvenir.

.   .   .   .   .

The rain was heavier when they got back on deck but Shannon was still there, ignoring the soaking his uniform was receiving, scorning the waterproofs donned by the seamen around him.

He waited, face expressionless, while Carrick spat out the scuba breathing tube and shoved back his face-mask.

"Cleared, sir," Carrick told him with a grin.

"Good." Shannon's voice sounded hoarse. "And no problems aboard, mister. A shade more seepage from one of the plates, but nothing we can't handle."

Stripping off his air tanks, Clapper Bell dumped them on the deck and gave a contented stretch.

"No bother at all," he said cheerfully. "Worked like an angel's kiss, the way I said, eh?"

"Like an angel's kiss?" Shannon blinked then rubbed a slow hand across his beard, wiping the rain clinging to it. There was another hint of moisture around his eyes, and he cleared his throat vigorously. "You're the hairiest looking angel I've ever seen, bo'sun. But well done."

Stumping quickly, almost embarrassedly over to the rail, he kept his back to them for a moment then turned.

"Next high water is at 03.16 hours. I'm going to wait till then. You can assemble a shore leave party after the evening meal, mister—include yourself and the bo'sun. You've earned it."

Hands in his pockets, he walked jauntily away, a strange sound coming from his lips.

Captain James Shannon was whistling.

CHAPTER SIX

Detective Inspector Jason arrived out by launch again as the fishery cruiser's crew were finishing their evening meal. Drenched by rain and spray, he stood on deck like a half-drowned, tweedy scarecrow until Shannon appeared and brought him to the 'tween decks wardroom.

Carrick was already there with Jumbo Wills, Pettigrew was summoned from the inevitable snooze in his cabin, and once Jason had a mug of coffee between his hands they chased the steward out of earshot.

"Not that there's much to tell," confessed Jason, a stray trickle of damp running down his face. He mopped it away. "Take the Halley Bay raid—while it was going on, everybody claims they were here in Port MacFarlane, at this damned wedding party. But don't expect any of them to remember who else was there."

"It was that kind of a night," agreed Jumbo Wills happily.

"I'd heard." The County man sipped his coffee morosely. "About the only thing that is even half certain is that Dan Fraser was still around when it finally died about four a.m." He glanced hopefully at Shannon. "Any luck with the list of boats you mentioned, Captain?"

"Nothing significant." Shannon shook his head reluctantly. "One or two are boats I wouldn't have expected in these waters, but with the wedding coming up—"

"Exactly." Jason scowled. "And when those lobsters are unloaded on the markets, who's to tell where they came from? This raid could be only a start—someone has come up with a sweet money-making idea."

"What about Christie's death?" asked Carrick quietly. "Do you still say murder, Inspector?"

"I don't say anything," countered Jason. He sipped his coffee again and shrugged defensively. "There's only the post-mortem report and—well, circumstance, I suppose, with those damned Fraser brothers again. Dan Fraser has a custom-tailored alibi that checks out. But I'm not so sure about his brother."

"Why?" asked Shannon, frowning.

"Because he has a damned weak story to account for the time between leaving Captain MacLean's place and getting back aboard the *Razorbill*." Jason rubbed another trickle of wet from his face, cursing in the process. "And he got back there just before the mob aboard realised what was happening on this side of the harbour." He paused. "Captain, how did the visitor who sabotaged your steering get aboard?"

Shannon shook his head. But Pettigrew leaned forward, his thin face unusually thoughtful.

"There's only one way," he declared in a weary, stating the obvious, voice. "Swim round from somewhere else in the harbour, then climb aboard. We'd only one man on gangway watch, half the crew ashore and most of the rest sleeping—it wouldn't be hard."

"And young Fraser is a pretty good swimmer," murmured Jason. He waited for comment, seemed disappointed when there was none, and sighed. "I'd like to know where the hell he is on this honeymoon cruise, but I'd get my knuckles rapped hard if I started any wholesale search of the Western Isles for one damned sailboat."

"And if you found him and dragged him back, you'd have to be right," mused Carrick. "Otherwise—'police persecution ruins honeymoon.' The newspapers would love it."

"Thanks," said the County man sarcastically. He gulped down the rest of his coffee. "Now it's about time I got back ashore. I've reports of my own to make."

"Inspector—" Jumbo Wills, who'd been fidgeting, cleared his throat awkwardly "—how about the watchman at Halley Bay? I found him pretty odd."

"Francie MacPhee?" Jason grinned a little as he pushed back his chair. "I wouldn't call him odd, just bloody awkward. But I don't think he's holding back." Rising, he began pulling on his dripping coat and asked over his shoulder. "Incidentally, what happened to that window at Captain MacLean's house?"

"Vandals," said Shannon curtly, with a warning glance to Carrick.

"There's plenty of that about." The County man wished them good evening and left, Shannon going with him.

As the wardroom door closed, Jumbo Wills twisted his freckled young face into a puzzled frown.

"The man's crazy," he said almost indignantly. "Roddy Fraser wouldn't kill anyone—not like that." Getting up, he gestured another protest at Carrick and Pettigrew. "Think on it. Would either of you go out and kill someone just before you were due to be married?"

"I might," grunted Pettigrew. "If he talked as much as you."

"Seriously—" began Wills, then sighed and gave up.

•   •   •   •   •

The shore leave party left aboard the cutter at nine p.m., huddled together in oilskins while the rain met them with a savage glee and an angry, chopping swell drenched the little boat's length in spray. By the time they reached harbour and scrambled ashore the first priority for most was shelter and a drink in the nearest bar.

Clapper Bell hung back for a moment, waiting for Carrick.

"Buy you one?" he suggested, another downpour pattering against his shoulders and upturned collar. "It's my turn."

"Maybe later." Carrick grinned his thanks. "But not right now."

The bo'sun blinked then understood.

"And the best of luck," he said with a wink. "Say hello for me while you're at it."

He trotted off after the other hurrying figures. There was a public telephone box outside the harbour offices and Carrick squeezed into its shelter, found some change, then lifted the receiver and dialled Jimsy MacLean's number. The telephone at the other end rang briefly, then Tara Grant's voice came on the line.

"Like to take pity on a half-drowned sailor?" he asked cheerfully.

She laughed. "Come on up, Webb. About all I'm doing is watching the rain."

"In two minutes," he promised and hung up.

The harbour master's car was still where he'd left it. With a murmured blessing in Benson's direction he climbed aboard, started the engine, then set it moving with the windscreen wipers slapping busily.

The rain was starting to ease a little as he turned the Ford into Ard-Tulach's driveway but he still had to sprint from the car to the shelter of the porch. Ringing the bell, he waited then was surprised when Jimsy MacLean opened the door.

"Come in," said MacLean curtly. "Don't bring too much of that wet with you."

Carrick entered the house and stripped off his soaked cap and dripping oilskins while the door slammed shut again.

"Shannon's still got himself stuck out there," said MacLean flatly. "How bad is it now?"

"We've blasted some of the reef away," answered Carrick, mopping his face with a handkerchief. "Next high water should tell."

As he put the handkerchief away he had his first clear glimpse of the man and had to fight down his surprise. In a few hours Jimsy MacLean seemed to have aged ten years. His thin face was grey and almost sick, his shoulders were hunched forward as if tired fighting some mysterious burden and all the previous bounce and energy seemed drained from his body.

"How about here?" asked Carrick quietly. "Any more trouble?"

"No." MacLean's one good eye glared at him in immediate anger. "I said I could handle things, Carrick. If you want to do me a favour then leave it at that—you and your captain."

"If he's still worried, it's because he's a friend," said Carrick neutrally. "I'm sorry I asked."

"No need." MacLean showed a slight remorse for a second, then it had gone. "But I can handle things on my own."

"If you think so," shrugged Carrick.

"I do." MacLean had begun struggling into a coat. "I've got

to go down to the village for a spell. But you didn't come for my company, anyway."

Buttoning the coat, picking up a scuffed leather brief-case from the hall table, he nodded briefly and went out into the rain. As the door closed again, Tara Grant arrived from the rear of the house, glanced at the table where the brief-case had been lying, and seemed puzzled.

"Has he gone already?" Her hair was tousled and she was still in her sweater and trousers. "He told me he'd be here for a spell."

"Maybe it was me," admitted Carrick. "I seem to have that effect on him."

"Everybody does at the moment." She grimaced but left it at that and gestured at her clothes. "I was going to change—I've been tidying Mhari's room and it has been some job. If I get you a drink, can you give me five minutes?"

He nodded easily then had an idea and added casually, "Turn me loose on that telescope in the turret room and you can make it ten."

"Fine." Tara smiled, relieved. "You know the way."

She poured him a whisky in the front room, where the broken window was still boarded up, then left him. Carrick sipped the drink for a moment and took the glass with him as he climbed the stairs. At the top, the door to the turret room was ajar and he went in, carefully closing the door behind him.

The telescope was still in position at the window but he ignored it, setting down the glass on MacLean's desk. A few household bills were lying on the desk-top and he glanced at them then tried the drawers.

The drawer above the knee-hole was locked, but the lock was small and old and simple. Lips pursed, he considered it for a moment then went over to a shelf and came back with a narrow-bladed knife with an ornate brass handle, a souvenir of some Indian Ocean trip. Working carefully with the tip of the blade, he got the leverage he needed and the lock clicked back.

Setting the knife down, Carrick opened the drawer. Jimsy Mac-Lean's personal papers lay inside in neat, orderly bundles and he checked them through quickly, disliking the task but telling himself it had to be done.

He found what he wanted in an old manilla envelope and emptied its contents on the desk-top.

There were almost a dozen notes, all written in block capitals and undated, scrawled on an assortment of sizes of paper, all on the same theme.

"It's share-out time on the *Dancella* salvage, Captain Jimsy," said one. He pushed beside another which spelled things out more tersely. "Pay up, Jimsy, or we collect our own way."

Sighing, he put them back in the envelope, returned the envelope to the drawer, and closed it again. The unlit fire-bomb tossed through MacLean's front window must have been just one more stage in a steady build-up of threats and pressures against the retired sailor, whatever kind of truth or fancy lay behind them.

Bending down with the knife again, he worked at closing the lock. That took a little time but at last it clicked into place. He stretched upright, relieved—and found Tara Grant standing in the opened doorway watching him, a loose housecoat over her shoulders, one hand clutching it tight at the neck, her face pale and her mouth a tight line of anger and contempt.

"Is burglary one of your sidelines?" she asked coldly.

"No." Setting down the knife, he met her icy gaze wryly. "But the way things are—"

"Don't bother explaining," she said bitterly. "I came to ask if you wanted to stay here or if we'd go out. Now you're leaving."

"Tara, wouldn't you like to know why?" asked Carrick wearily.

"You used me to get up here and you were trying to open that desk. It's enough." She drew a deep, bitter breath. "All right, I won't tell him. He's worried enough. But get out, Webb—now."

There was no sense in trying to argue. Nodding, he put the knife back where he'd found it, finished his drink in a gulp, then went past her. At least, as far as Tara Grant was concerned, he hadn't been inside that drawer.

She followed him out of the room then down to the half-landing below. But she stayed there while he went the rest of the way to the front door. Once he'd put on his hat and oilskins he glanced back. She was still up there, her face the same tight, angry mask.

"Goodnight, Tara," he said quietly, and went out.

.   .   .   .   .

Port MacFarlane's tiny main street was glistening with rain as the station wagon drove back along it. In a pensive mood, Carrick slowed as he saw the village hotel ahead then parked outside. He sat with the engine off for a moment, still thinking, then gave up with a sigh and climbed out of the car.

Inside the hotel, the main bar was noisy and crowded. He chose the quieter cocktail lounge and was heading for one of the bar stools when he was hailed from a corner. Sitting alone at a table, Dirk Peters waved him over.

"On your own?" Peters shoved out a chair, beckoning the barmaid as Carrick sat down. "What are you drinking, Carrick?"

He asked for a whisky. Peters ordered the same, paid for the drinks when they came, then grinned at him.

"Your ship's beginning to look like part of the scenery out on that reef. What's the situation now?"

Carrick shrugged. "We're waiting on the next high water. That might do it." Lighting a cigarette, he looked at the stockily built marina owner with a mild curiosity. "I didn't know you were back in harbour."

"We got back a couple of hours ago." Peters rubbed his broken nose and chuckled. "Farrell and I spent the day using the *San Helena* as a fishing boat—big game rod and line style, or that was how it was supposed to be. Farrell caught himself a fair-sized tunny, but all I kept hooking were dogfish." He shrugged philosophically. "Still, Farrell's got the itch for more—he wants us out again at first light tomorrow."

"With any luck, you'll have a clear channel down the loch by then," said Carrick, trying to appear interested.

"And you'll be back in business?"

"Not till we've had a full damage survey."

Peters nodded, rubbing a pattern on the table with one hand. "Your captain has my sympathy, Carrick. That sort of thing isn't

supposed to happen to fishery cruisers—the nautical Eleventh
Commandment. But who'll cope with the Halley Bay raid while
you're patching up?"

Carrick shrugged. "The County police are handling most of it.
Why?"

"Just that maybe they should keep an eye on things out there,"
mused Peters.

"Meaning?"

"That old watchman MacPhee." Peters lowered his voice a
shade. "One of my crew came back with a story that MacPhee
could have trouble heading his way. The lobster fishermen have
got hold of the notion that he was in on the raid and took that
tap on the head as part of his alibi."

"Anything else?" asked Carrick, frowning.

Peters nodded. "They're talking of sorting him out in their own
way."

"That wouldn't be too clever," said Carrick sharply.

"My feelings." Peters stopped and glanced past him. Two new-
comers had entered the room. One was Clapper Bell, who gave
Carrick a wave then headed straight for the bar. The other, a
hatchet-faced man in slacks and a waterproof anorak, hesitated
then came towards them as Dirk Peters beckoned.

"Harry Tessin, our skipper on the *San Helena*," said Peters
briefly as the man arrived. "Harry, this is the chief officer from the
fishery cruiser."

Tessin nodded briefly, dragging a slip of paper from an inside
pocket.

"This was radioed in for you, Mr. Peters," he said, handing it
over. "I thought it looked urgent."

"Oh?" Peters scanned the message and pursed his lips. "It is.
Harry, I'll come back with you." Remembering Carrick, he
shrugged apologetically. "Business—and it needs an answer."

The two men left. Clapper Bell waited a moment or two then
wandered over from the bar with a pint of beer in one hand and
sat in the chair Peters had vacated.

"That wasn't the kind of company I thought you were organis-
ing," said the bo'sun with an amiable curiosity. "What went
wrong?"

"The other possibility came unstuck," said Carrick dryly.

"Hard luck." Bell's rugged faced showed no particular sympathy. "But if you're going to kill time with the *San Helena* bunch, watch your pockets."

Carrick raised an eyebrow and waited.

"She's carryin' six of a crew. I bought a couple o' them a drink an' they're rough material—very rough, straight from the bottom of the heap." Bell left it at that. "Still, before that I was gossipin' with some of the local skippers. There's a thing or two that might interest the Old Man, though it cost me a few rounds—"

"Using somebody else's money, probably," nodded Carrick. "Well?"

"MacPhee the watchman out at Halley Bay—" Bell paused, frowning a little "—they've got hold of the notion he could tell a lot more if he wanted. One or two think it might be an idea to try an' thump it out of him."

"I heard that from Peters," agreed Carrick thoughtfully. "They might have reason, Clapper. MacPhee has something worrying him."

"I'd tow him round the bay at the end o' a rope myself if they're right," said Bell reasonably. "But it was a couple o' things I heard about the man that seemed to maybe matter."

"What kind of things?" Carrick tossed him a cigarette and lit one himself.

"Well, that it was Captain MacLean who got him the job as watchman out there. An' that the reason was MacPhee served with him on his last ship, the one that brought in that tanker."

"You're sure?" Carrick sat bolt upright.

"The locals are—an' they reckon the reason Captain MacLean is goin' round like he had a red-hot needle up his backside is he thinks MacPhee sold out too." Bell looked at him curiously. "Do you think it might fit, sir?"

"In a whole lot of ways." Carrick shoved back his chair and rose. "Clapper, I'm driving over to Halley Bay. It's time I had another talk with MacPhee."

"Want me to come?" queried Bell hopefully. "He could have company, the unfriendly kind."

"That might even help," said Carrick grimly. "But you stay, Clapper. Just keep drifting around—you're doing fine."

.　　　.　　　.　　　.　　　.

The rain had died to a light drizzle by the time the station wagon topped the last rise before Halley Bay. But it was still heavily overcast and the night was shaping fast towards an early dusk.

Flicking the gearchange into neutral, Carrick coasted down towards the huts with the Ford's engine ticking over. He stopped it beside a massive pile of empty lobster boxes, got out quietly and looked around, puzzled. Once again the place seemed deserted. The workboat still lay at the water's edge, the sea murmuring against her stern. A few gulls strutted the sand. But the rest was silence.

Walking over to the nearest hut, he swung open the door and glanced in. It was a storeroom, filled with ropes and floats and other gear. Shrugging, he crunched over to the other hut and tried the door. It opened with a loud creak and he stepped into the dull, heavily shadowed interior then stopped, mouth tightening.

Francie MacPhee's living quarters looked as if a miniature tornado had passed through. Chairs were wrecked, the table had been overturned, tins and cooking pots from a broken shelf littered the wooden floor. The drawers of a small dressing chest lay open, clothing hanging from them as if raked through and abandoned.

But there was no sign of MacPhee. Threading his way forward through the chaos, Carrick saw a small, dark pool on the floor beside the dressing chest. It was blood, and a trail of smaller splashes and smears led from there towards an old camp bed but stopped just short of reaching it, ending in another pool of blood.

Carrick stared down at it grimly, wondering what had happened in the hut from that point.

Then the door behind him creaked—and he swung round as two men sprang at him through the gloom. A club like a sawn-off pick-haft swung down and grazed his shoulder as he side-stepped but the second man, similarly armed, used his weapon like a lance-point and pain slammed through Carrick's ribs as it connected.

Stumbling back, he tensed as they closed in, two purposeful, silent figures clad in fisherman jerseys and overalls, stocking masks over their heads. The clubs rose again, and he snatched up a broken chair-back and swung it desperately.

The chair-back splintered against the nearest man's face, bringing a scream of agony and sending him reeling. The other attacker hesitated a vital fraction of a second and, abandoning the shattered chair-back, Carrick lunged in a shoulder-charge which slammed the man back and sent him sprawling over the camp bed.

Then the first man was shambling in again, though with less enthusiasm. Dodging a wild blow, Carrick slammed a fist deep into the man's stomach, saw him fold with a whoop of pain, then in turn was brought crashing to the floor as the other figure catapulted back into the fight.

They rolled, locked together in a wild fury of blows and kicks. On top for a moment, Carrick wrenched himself clear and tried to rise—then stopped as an arm locked round his throat from behind and a needle-sharp knife point jabbed under his chin.

"Freeze," snarled a new voice in his ear.

The knife jabbing again forced him to obey and the stocking-masked figure on the floor wriggled clear, panting for breath. The second man was leaning against the wall, moaning, but the newcomer behind Carrick didn't relax that strangle-hold throat lock.

"Up," came the hoarse command. "Slowly."

Helpless, Carrick did as he'd been told. When he tried to turn his head, the knife jabbed again.

"You had to stick your nose in, didn't you?" growled the man behind him.

There was a rustle of movement, he glimpsed one of the stocking-masked figures swinging a pick-haft at his head . . . then all he knew was an explosion of pain and fire which merged into a tunnel of velvet black.

. . . . .

He came to again lying on the floor, face down, with an evil-smelling gag rammed in his mouth and his hands tied behind his back. He discovered his feet were tied too, his head throbbed with pain at the slightest move, his ribs hurt, and for a few moments he stayed as he was, fighting down an almost overwhelming nausea.

At last, with an effort, Carrick rolled over on his left side. It had become dark outside and a pale edge of moonlight coming through a grimy window showed a foraging rat scurrying back into hiding at his unexpected movement.

The hut was empty, the door lying open, and all he could hear was the distant murmur of the sea. Another wave of nausea hit him then passed, and he slowly dragged his way across the floor to the camp bed. When he got there, it needed a few attempts before he was able to heave into a sitting position with his back against the bed.

Fumbling blindly, he located one of the metal bed-legs and ran his fingers along it until he found a roughened, jagged edge on the angle-iron. Cursing the way the rope bit into his wrists, he began the slow, awkward job of sawing the strands up and down against the roughened edge.

It was slow, monotonous work and he'd been at it almost twenty minutes, with a long way to go, when he heard a car engine approaching. Soon headlights swept briefly across the open door of the hut, the car braked outside, and its doors opened and closed.

There were footsteps outside, a man's voice called, then a torch shone in the doorway. It swept round the hut and stopped, pinning him in its beam.

He heard a grunt which was almost a chuckle then another figure pushed forward and hurried over. Tara Grant knelt beside him in the torchlight and, pale-faced, quickly undid the gag. Spitting it out, Carrick found he couldn't speak for a moment.

"Are you all right?" she demanded anxiously.

"More or less," he managed thickly.

"Dirk." She swung round. "Don't just stand there."

"Sorry." Peters ambled over, set down the torch, and produced a clasp-knife. The blade slashed through the ropes at Carrick's

118

wrists and ankles then the man considered him with a sardonic interest.

"What the hell happened to you?" he demanded.

"I arrived at the wrong time, that's all." Carrick stopped and winced as the circulation began to return to his limbs. He rubbed his wrists first, sucking his teeth for a moment against the pain. "The other visitors played rough."

"There's blood on your head," said Tara slowly. She peered closer then glanced at Peters. "Dirk, couldn't we get some more light?"

Peters found an oil lantern, lit it, and looked around as it cast its glow. He whistled softly at the confusion of broken, overturned furniture.

"Looks like I was right about what might happen to MacPhee," he commented mildly. "Where is he anyway?"

"I didn't get a chance to find out." Carrick switched his massaging from wrists to ankles and grinned at Tara, who was still kneeling beside him. "In fact, I walked straight into trouble—which wasn't being very clever."

She managed an answering smile and rose. "At least you're still in one piece. But that head wound needs bathing."

While Tara went over to a water tap and basin in the far corner, Peters put a surprisingly strong arm round Carrick's shoulders and helped him sit on the camp bed. Carrick nodded his thanks, took the cigarette Peters offered, and drew on it gladly once it was lit.

"What brought you here?" he asked wryly after a moment.

"The lady." Peters glanced towards Tara, who was coming back with a dampened cloth. "It was her idea."

Puzzled, Carrick let her begin dabbing at the wound on his head. But she said nothing.

"Why?" he asked after a moment.

"I came down to the village looking for you." She worked on, carefully avoiding meeting his gaze, her voice low and awkward. "I—well, your friend the bo'sun said you'd left for here—"

"Then I found her getting ready to drive after you on her own. That's when I suggested I'd maybe better come along," finished

Peters. He lit a cigarette of his own then gestured around. "The thing is, what do we do now?"

"MacPhee might be lying outside somewhere," said Carrick grimly.

"Uh-huh." Peters rubbed one side of his squashed nose and considered the point unemotionally. "Well, I'd better be the one who does the looking."

He picked up the torch and went out, closing the door. Carrick drew on his cigarette again then, as Tara finished reached out and took her hand.

"Thanks," he said quietly. "But after what happened—"

"I—I decided maybe I was wrong," she said slowly. "That's why I wanted to find you. I still couldn't have let you open that desk, but—"

"But I'm a well-meaning rat?" Carrick chuckled without malice, got to his feet and steadied himself for a moment against the wall. "Well, that's at least one bright spot in this mess."

"If I hadn't thrown you out, some of it might not have happened," she reminded bitterly, then looked around the hut. "Who would do it, Webb? Dirk says the fishermen were planning something—"

"They were talking. There's a hell of a difference." Carrick glanced at his watch. It was close to eleven-thirty and at least half an hour had passed since he'd been attacked. Half an hour in which the men could have travelled a long way—by sea or road. "Old MacPhee's the one I'm worried about now. At best, he's out there somewhere hurt and scared."

"And at worst?"

He shrugged but was saved from answering as the door opened and Peters returned.

"Any luck?" asked Carrick.

"Nothing." Peters shook his head. "I checked all round, then down along the beach. He's not anywhere here."

A telephone was lying under the overturned table but the instrument was dead, the wires cut at the wall socket. When they went outside, Carrick found the station wagon where he'd left it— but all four tyres had been slashed.

"Nice people," murmured Peters.

Carrick nodded, wondering what a certain harbour master was going to say when he heard.

That left Tara's sports car. They crammed aboard the two-seater, Tara driving, and left the huts. About a mile along the road a light on a hillside led them along a small track to a crofter's cottage.

The crofter was young and married, had a telephone, and at first thought there had been a road accident. But he left them alone while Carrick telephoned the police station at Tobermory and located Detective Inspector Jason.

When Jason came on the line, Carrick kept his story to a bare, factual outline of what had happened at Halley Bay. At the finish, Jason muttered to someone at his end of the line for a moment then spoke to Carrick again.

"All right, I'm sending a car-load of men there now," he said wearily. "That's all I can spare. Tell Captain Shannon I'll be along in the morning. And Carrick, do me a favour—don't let anything else go wrong before then. The County can't afford the overtime."

The distant receiver slammed down. The crofter said nothing, but produced a bottle and glasses. Carrick's drink was twice as large as the rest—raw, hill-still whisky which burned away the last of his aches and giddiness.

Then they left and were back in Port MacFarlane half an hour after midnight. Peters climbed out first once Tara stopped the little car at the harbour.

"Time for bed," he said with a twisted grin. "Carrick, tomorrow's fishing is going to seem dull now."

He ambled off towards the *San Helena*'s berth. Turning to Tara Carrick looked at her in silence for a moment.

"You haven't asked why I went to Halley Bay," he said at last.

She frowned. "You knew about the fishermen. I thought—"

"Wrong." He leaned an elbow on the dashboard and shook his head. "I went to see MacPhee because he sailed with Jimsy Mac-Lean when MacLean towed in the *Dancella*."

"The oil tanker?" She looked at him blankly. "But you can't think—"

"Right now I can't think very straight about anything," he confessed. "But I wouldn't advise you to ask Captain Jimsy any pointed questions."

"I won't."

"Good." He kissed her gently on the lips. "If you want to help him, stay out of his way—but keep your eyes open."

She nodded.

Carrick climbed out of the car, watched while it pulled away, then turned and walked round the harbour to where *Marlin's* leave boat was waiting. Most of the men were already aboard and the last, including Clapper Bell, arrived within a few minutes.

"How did it go with MacPhee, sir?" asked Bell, squeezing into a space beside him on the centre thwart while the launch was cast off and began growling its way out of harbour.

"Rough," said Carrick shortly.

"Interesting rough?" The bo'sun raised a hopeful eyebrow.

Carrick nodded but left it at that. It could keep till they were aboard, when he'd also have to tell Shannon.

The launch began to pitch as they passed the breakwater and soon they were being drenched in spray again. Jammed between Bell and one of the engine-room squad who insisted on trying to sing, Carrick hardly noticed it.

First there had been the fisherman Christie, now, in all probability, Francie MacPhee was dead. Somebody, somewhere, was either ruthless or desperate.

He tried to think round it. But the throb of the engine began synchronising with the throb starting up again in his head, and he gave up.

. . . . .

High water at 03.16 hours brought exactly two inches more tide than the standard tables predicted, and it was enough. At the first attempt and with power in hand, Her Majesty's fishing cruiser *Marlin* grated free from the reef and became a ship again.

There was no audience ashore to see her crawl back into Port

MacFarlane and the pumps were working again as she berthed, combating a new leak which had started in the forepeak. Another hour passed while Pettigrew's damage control party cursed and toiled before her crew could snatch some rest, but when they slept it was with a relieved certainty that their luck had turned.

Some of that dissipated in the morning. The Department's flotilla survey officer, Lieutenant Commander Logan—a grey-faced man who had collected his rank as a hostilities only officer in World War Two and refused to let anyone forget it—arrived at the harbour driving a Land-Rover with Fishery Protection badges on its doors.

He came aboard with a scowl and a brief-case, saw Captain Shannon briefly, then disappeared below with Jumbo Wills as a somewhat nervous escort. They reappeared after an hour, Logan staying in the wardroom long enough to eat a silent breakfast before he vanished back to his task.

Detective Inspector Jason was next at nine a.m. and went straight to Captain Shannon's day-cabin. A full half-hour passed before a messenger summoned Carrick to join them, and he arrived to find the County man and *Marlin*'s commander facing each other across a table like two dogs who had just finished the first round of a quarrel over a newly discovered bone.

"Mister, I've given Inspector Jason a rundown on most of what we know to date—and explaining to him there's been no deliberate withholding of information," rasped Shannon with a flat emphasis. "When I say most, that includes what has been happening to Captain MacLean. I've explained our reasons."

"You mean you've told me there's damned all I can do about them," corrected Jason bleakly. He dug his hands deep into the pockets of his baggy tweed jacket as if it helped. "I wouldn't exactly call that co-operation."

A wintry smile flickered across Shannon's bearded face then had gone.

"Well, let's say we're in agreement about the next stage," he said blandly. "Mainly because Inspector Jason hasn't anything better to offer."

Jason flushed but nodded.

"MacPhee can't be found," he admitted. "All we've got are a load of footprints on the sand near those damned huts at Halley Bay and what might be where a small boat was dragged ashore. But MacPhee or the three hard cases who attacked you—" he shook his head.

"So we've agreed on a joint effort," said Shannon, his eyes on Carrick. "The County police will concentrate on the MacPhee business and continue trying to find out more about what happen to Christie—but playing both quietly. Captain MacLean will be left to us for the moment, and the same goes for the lobster raid."

"Unless the whole damned lot are in one package," said Jason, attempting a stubborn rearguard action. "That's the part I don't like. If it wasn't for the spread of this thing—hell, I even got involved with the telephone people this morning. Asking them to repair the 'phone at that hut again. Twice in 24 hours—they loved that, believe me." He sighed. "If I wasn't so blasted short of men—"

"But you are," said Shannon smoothly. "And we're glad to help."

Lips pursed, the policeman nodded.

"Just remember that I still want to get my hands on young Roddy Fraser," he said bitterly. "And exactly what do you plan to do about MacLean?"

"Captain MacLean," corrected Shannon mildly, a magnanimous victor. "All we can until he makes some kind of formal complaint, Inspector—talk to him again and keep an eye on him. But—ah—I've a notion or two."

"I hope they're good enough." Jason surveyed them morosely. "Captain, what would you say if I told you how to run your ship?"

"I'm a polite man," said Shannon impassively. "Probably I'd just ignore you."

Sighing, Jason gave up. He said goodbye and left a moment later and Shannon gave a short, barking laugh once the cabin door had shut.

"Right, mister," he said abruptly. "Now we can get on with things—starting with Jimsy MacLean."

Going over to the desk, *Marlin's* captain returned with a thin file of papers and dropped them on the table with a satisfied grunt.

"The *Dancella* salvage summary—at last. Lieutenant Commander Logan brought it." He scowled for a moment. "And that's about the only reason I'm glad he came. From the way he acts, he was fathered by a slide-rule. But this summary, mister—there was a row about what happened, though it was kept quiet."

"Share-out trouble?" Carrick found it hard to believe. Crew shares on most types of marine salvage were based on a time-honoured formula, with something for every man involved down to the most junior hand. "I thought—"

"Let me tell it," said Shannon with a touch of irritation. "When Jimsy MacLean found the *Dancella* most of her crew had abandoned ship—but the tanker captain and a couple of his men were still aboard. The captain stayed on his own once Jimsy had put a boat's crew aboard." He paused and gave an odd sniff. "Then by a strange coincidence the *Dancella's* captain—ah—slipped and fell and knocked himself out, so Jimsy had him shipped off too."

Carrick shaped a silent whistle, with an idea what was coming. As long as the *Dancella's* captain had been on the tanker it hadn't been abandoned. But once he left, the salvage money Jimsy MacLean could claim would have soared.

"You've guessed it, mister." Shannon gave an almost imperceptible nod. "Jimsy MacLean was on the *Dancella* when it happened—and the *Dancella's* captain couldn't remember falling afterwards. He had more a notion he'd been thumped on the head. Except, of course, Jimsy MacLean had most of his boat's crew as witnesses ready to swear to it on a stack of Bibles."

"Including MacPhee?"

"Including MacPhee. But I didn't tell Inspector Jason that little story—he can wait until I've heard Jimsy's version." Shannon prowled the cabin for a moment then turned to face Carrick again. "Now, your turn—there's a naval helicopter arriving at ten hundred hours. You'll fly with the pilot as observer, standard search pattern within a thirty mile radius of here. I want those lobster rafts found—but don't forget we've promised Jason we'll try to locate Roddy Fraser's boat. Any questions?"

Carrick shook his head.

Ten a.m. left him just enough time to explain to the harbour master about his station wagon. And he didn't particularly want to hang around after that. . . .

CHAPTER SEVEN

The promised helicopter, a small anti-submarine Westland Wasp with Royal Navy markings, appeared over Port MacFarlane on schedule and touched down on a cleared stretch of quayside. Rotor blades chunking, it stayed there long enough for Carrick to scramble aboard, strap in, and pull on the padded helmet the pilot, a grinning young sub-lieutenant, handed him. Then the sound of the powerful Bristol Sidderley Nimbus engine changed, the rotor blades quickened to a shimmer, and they were airborne.

"This is Fishery Protection's show," shouted the pilot above the chunking beat as they headed down Loch Rudha. "So where do we start?"

Carrick settled for a western sweep, and the helicopter swung obediently. At about two hundred feet above the sea, following the line of every indentation, they checked their way down the Mull coastline until the island of Iona showed ahead then swung out and began a regular search pattern of the smaller islands.

On some, the helicopter's arrival sent sheep stampeding for shelter or caused grey seals to go plunging into the sea. Several times they circled or came down low, the rotors' downrush of air fanning the waves, while they checked on what turned out to be drifting flotsam or the sunken outline of an old wreck.

When it was Horsehead Island's turn, Carrick made a particularly careful check. But it was difficult. The high, black cliffs cast deep shadows and rough seas were breaking on shoal rocks creamed over a considerable area. The *Razorbill* was in at the landing stage and there were men working around the lobster storage pool. They looked up stonily as the helicopter passed overhead, then returned to their tasks.

After that there were more islands, occasional shipping or little groups of fishing boats at work, once a great, black-finned school of basking sharks lazing on the surface and a little later a false alarm which brought them down to discover a drifting mass of weed.

The pilot's name was Mike. Normally, he operated from a frigate and his Wasp helicopter, with a three hundred mile range, would have been weaponed with two 270 lb torpedoes. Munching a chocolate bar, he made it clear that the day's assignment rated as a holiday trip.

But he still kept his eyes open. They'd left the slim white tower of Skerryvore lighthouse behind and were working up the east side of Tiree towards the grassy outline of Coll when he suddenly thumbed to his right.

A white motor yacht lay two miles ahead. The Wasp swung towards it and in a few minutes Carrick was looking down on the *San Helena*, cruising slowly and with a small group of figures clustered near her stern. One of the men waved a greeting and as the helicopter hovered lower Carrick recognised Frank Farrell.

"Okay?" queried the pilot.

Carrick nodded and the Wasp headed off, climbing again. When he looked back, the *San Helena* was still on the same course.

"That's the life," commented the pilot enviously. "Sail on, gallant captain, and where's the drink I ordered. What's she doing out here?"

"Fishing," answered Carrick vaguely, though he'd noticed the fishing chairs at her stern had been empty. "At least, that was the programme they had in mind."

"Sounds like you've been mixing with the moneyed classes." The pilot grinned then forgot about it, heading for the next little island on their horizon.

After two hours' flying time the Wasp's fuel gauge read low. They headed back to the Mull coastline, gained height to clear the hills, and a little later lowered down on the grass landing strip at Glen Forsa.

The Wasp had been expected. As they switched off and climbed out a refuelling truck was driving over. A couple of small private aircraft were parked nearby and a twin-engined freight 'plane was being loaded near the airstrip's administration huts.

Leaving the Wasp's pilot to supervise its refuelling, Carrick walked towards the huts. The freight 'plane was being loaded with lobster boxes from a truck, and the two airstrip loaders doing the work nodded a greeting but didn't slow their steady rhythm. Curious, Carrick checked one of the boxes and grimaced at the "R and D Fraser" consignment label.

"Bound for London, that lot," said an unexpected voice behind him. He turned, surprised, and Clapper Bell came nearer, grinning. For the first time, Carrick noticed that the grey Fishery Protection Land-Rover which had arrived that morning was parked beside one of the huts.

"That damage survey bloke wanted some extra gear collected off a 'plane that's comin' in," explained the bo'sun, hands in his pockets. "I drew the job. How were things wi' the whirleybird, sir?"

"Dull." Carrick thought of the couple of routine progress reports the pilot had radioed back. By now, Captain Shannon had probably written off the helicopter exercise as one more waste of time. "What's it been like on *Marlin?*"

Clapper Bell shrugged dispassionately. "The buzz is we'll need to spend about a week on repairs an' then head for a dockyard. The Old Man has other ideas, but—"

"He can't win them all." Carrick considered the lobster boxes again. "Got a knife, Clapper?"

Puzzled, the bo'sun produced a heavy-bladed seaman's clasp-knife. Using it, Carrick levered open a box lid. Inside was cool and damp and tightly packed with lobsters and he lifted out the nearest. While it wriggled feebly in his grip he checked the claws. Each had been immobilised with a tiny plastic plug like the type he'd seen used on Horsehead Island. Shrugging, he returned the lobster to its place and hammered the lid in position again.

"Just a notion I had," he explained wryly.

Understanding, Clapper Bell nodded then gave a grunt. "Well, good luck to whoever buys that lot. I wouldn't, an' that's for sure."

"Meaning what?" Carrick raised an eyebrow.

"There are lobsters an' lobsters, right?" said Bell with a terse in-dignation. "I—uh—well, I brought back a couple o' Fraser's from Horsehead Island yesterday."

"Oh?" Carrick considered the bo'sun thoughtfully. "You for-got to mention it. Were they handing out samples?"

"Well—" for a moment Bell looked uncomfortable "—I just decided they wouldn't miss a couple, like. Then when we got back to *Marlin* I dumped them in a pail. Cook an' me were goin' to share them for lunch today." He shrugged sadly. "Then I took a decent look at them this mornin' an' dumped them over the side."

"What had gone off—you, or the lobsters?" queried Carrick with a grin.

"The lobsters, in a big way," said Bell heavily. "Both o' them had gone over-ripe or somethin' around the tail. Cook said it was some damned disease called Red Tail."

Carrick's grin faded, and he whistled. Once he'd been on a brief course with Fisheries Research. Most of the time the talk had been far above his head, but some of it had stuck—including Red Tail, for which he and a couple of other visiting protection cruiser officers had created a cruder definition, to be applied to their respective captains.

But to a lobster fisherman there was nothing funny about Red Tail. It was a low-grade bacterial infection which could decimate a lobster population, spreading like an epidemic. Though it usu-ally only occurred in the warmest of weather or in closed condi-tions. The thought ran on—closed conditions like the storage pool at Horsehead Island, if anything had gone wrong with the tidal flow which should have cleansed it twice daily . . .

"Better give me that knife again," he said slowly.

This time the two airstrip loaders stopped and watched, frown-ing, while they opened the same lobster box and checked its con-tents. All the lobsters inside seemed healthy enough.

They checked a second and a third, with the same result then shrugged at each other.

"Mind if we get on wi' things, Mac?" asked one of the loaders impatiently. "This 'plane has a schedule to meet."

"We're finished." Carrick closed the boxes again and signalled Clapper Bell to follow. They walked over towards the Land-Rover, then he asked, "Clapper, did you mention this to anyone else?"

"Didn't seem any reason." Bell frowned, instantly on guard. "I mean, a couple o' lobsters—"

"I don't care if you came back with a hundred," said Carrick wearily. "But we could have used the two you heaved overboard, believe me. When you get back, better tell the Old Man about them. And before he asks, tell him I'll take another look at Horsehead Island this afternoon."

Lips pursed and puzzled, Bell nodded. A moment later, the bo'sun had other things to do as a light aircraft landed and a messenger from the control hut told him it was the one he'd been waiting on.

Carrick walked back to meet the helicopter's pilot. He was thinking hard, thinking of a chain of possibilities which might begin with how the Frasers would react to the suddenly discovered blow that their hard-won, vital stock of lobsters were infected and likely to be worthless within a matter of days.

Leaving them with delivery orders in hand, a crew to be paid, boat payments to meet and a second new boat on order—and a quick solution to it all lying just across the water at Halley Bay.

Yet even that left major gaps. And was it the kind of solution the Frasers could consider worth one man's death and maybe a second killing?

·　　·　　·　　·　　·

He had a quick snack with the helicopter pilot and then they took off again. There was still an area to the north-west to be covered, from the scatter of tiny Treshnish Isles to the mainland bulk of Ardnamurchan Point. But that, Carrick reckoned, stretched the practical limits for their search to the maximum.

Near Ardnamurchan they saw a small motor sailer plunging along under full sail. Remembering Roddy Fraser, he had the

Wasp swoop down to investigate. But it was another boat, with totally different lines and a baby's washing fluttering at the stern. The yachtsman shook a fist at them for the things the rotors' wash was doing to his sails, and they veered off again.

They came back to Horsehead Island in mid-afternoon and saw the *Razorbill* still tied alongside the old landing stage but none of her crew visible. Tapping the pilot on the shoulder, Carrick gestured downward and the Wasp lost height as they began a slow, hovering anti-clockwise circuit of the black basalt cliffs.

The sun's angle cast new shadows from those of the morning and the sea had lessened. Peering down at the lapping waves, Carrick had a sense of hopelessness at the size of the task he'd been given. Even if the lobster rafts were anywhere near, they could have been weighed down and sunk, camouflaged over—any one of a dozen different tricks might mean he'd already passed over them.

If they were there at all.

They were more than halfway round the island, on its southerly end, when he was jerked out of his gloom. Down below, about fifty yards out from the base of another sheer cliff, a vague, wavering shape showed beneath the water. Little more than a discoloration, at the same time it was too regular in shape to be natural. He shouted in the pilot's ear and they stayed hovering over the spot for a moment while he tried to make up his mind.

But guesswork couldn't count. Tight-lipped, he took his bearings from the cliff and the distant mainland then nodded and the helicopter soared, heading for Port MacFarlane.

Fifteen minutes later he was on the quayside watching the Wasp take off again, this time heading back towards its base. For the sub-lieutenant, a day's unusual diversion was over. But for Carrick, the next stage lay ahead.

.   .   .   .   .

Aboard *Marlin*, Captain Shannon was in a bitter session with Lieutenant Commander Logan in the chartroom. When it finished, the Department survey man stalked off past Carrick with a poker face but with eyes that were hard and angry. Shannon was pretty much the same for a moment then boiled over.

"Mister, if I ever get closer to murder than right now it will be a damn-blasted miracle!" The round, bearded face exuded wrath. "A chinless, desk-bound wonder who does a handful of years in some damned wartime dockyard stamping ration coupons for all I know and thinks that makes him a seaman. You know what he asked me?"

"Sir?" Carrick waited woodenly.

. "On reflection, did I still feel I exercised proper judgement in my actions before we stranded?" Shannon opened and closed his mouth a couple of times in speechless rage then managed to go on. "Well, I told him. I told him what I thought of his questions, his attitude, his—well, of every damned thing about him except his father and mother. They're probably both unknown."

The outburst seemed to leave him feeling better. Leaning against the chartroom table, he shrugged with a grim despair.

"What didn't help, mister, was seeing Jimsy MacLean this morning. I put the story about the tanker salvage business to him, straight—and he told me to mind my own damned business then more or less threw me out. Stupid old goat—"

"You tried, sir," said Carrick wryly, glad he hadn't been aboard when Shannon came back from that particular mission.

"I tried. That would make a damned good epitaph," grunted Shannon. "What about you? I had Clapper Bell along about those lobsters and he said you were going to take another circle around Horsehead Island." He raised a heavy, questioning eyebrow. "Well?"

"There's a possibility to check out, sir," said Carrick. Seeing Shannon's immediate interest, he added quickly: "But it's a diving job."

"I see." Shannon considered for a moment. "All right, take the cutter and a landing party. Do the job properly—even if you've got to crack a few skulls in the process."

Stubbornly, Carrick shook his head. "That should maybe wait, sir. I'd rather try to get out quietly, then be sure of what's down there before we get to the skull-cracking bit."

"It seems everybody has taken to questioning my judgement today," said Shannon vindictively, scrubbing a hand across his beard. But he nodded. "Do it your way, then. Take a radio, mister—I want to know exactly what's out there the moment you're sure."

.   .   .   .

Ninety minutes later, crouching in the rubber packboat with Clapper Bell, close under the cliffs of Horsehead Island and being tossed and heaved with each new swell, Webb Carrick spared a moment to wonder if it wouldn't have been easier Shannon's way.

So far, he hadn't wasted time. As soon as he'd left the chartroom he'd collected Clapper Bell and ten minutes had been enough to gather all the gear they required, change into their scuba suits, and get the packboat into the water.

Once clear of Loch Rudha they'd opened up the big outboard and the packboat had gone creaming its way down the coast till they were well below Horsehead Island. Then, engine throttled back to little more than a murmur, no tell-tale white wake behind them, they'd made the crossing in a slow, curving route.

The packboat was small and dark enough to almost blend with the sea, the technique one Fishery Protection used often enough to steal up towards a fishing boat suspected of poaching. And even if someone had been deliberately patrolling the cliffs above it would have taken exceptionally keen eyes to spot their approach.

But now was different. The outboard was switched off and Clapper Bell was maintaining their position with a combination of a small sea-anchor and one of the packboat's emergency paddles. For once, he didn't appear particularly happy as Carrick shrugged his way into his aqualung harness.

"Maybe I should come down wi' you," he suggested again. "The boat won't drift far, sir—or we could take her right in an' moor, then swim out."

"Wouldn't work, Clapper." Carrick spat into his face-mask then rinsed the result over the side—the best de-misting combination known for face-mask glass. "I want to be sure there's a boat still up here, even if the Fraser crew come calling. A quick look then back up, that's all I'm doing."

Ignoring the bo'sun's muttered reply, he checked the cliff again. At sea level, it was impossible to spot the shimmer of sunken colour he'd seen from the helicopter but the position seemed right.

"Ready?" he queried.

"You're the boss," shrugged Bell. "Don't blame me if a couple o' thousand lobsters take a fancy to you."

He gave the bo'sun a brief grin, pulled down the face-mask, gripped the scuba's breathing tube between his teeth, and went over the side. Floating there for a moment, getting used to the first chill of the water, he finally duck-dived and began finning down towards the bottom.

The charts showed deep water close in against Horsehead Island, and as usual the charts were right. The depth gauge strapped to his left wrist was quivering at over seventy feet when Carrick reached the top fronds of a forest of lazily waving kelp weed.

He stopped there, swallowing hard to clear the pain mounting in his ears again, then leaked some air from the corner of his mouth into the face-mask to ease its pressure against his face. The demand regulator clicking reassuringly, the plume of bubbles from the outlet tube rising steadily and still likely to be seen by Clapper Bell above, Carrick looked around.

There was only the weed, a few pinnacles of rock and the inevitable myriad of tiny, darting fish, but he hadn't expected to be lucky first time. Taking the direction from the compass on his other wrist, he began swimming roughly parallel with the line of the cliff. Counting as he went, he stopped at forty then went back the way he'd come and tried from there in the opposite direction.

The count was close to the limit again when the same strange shimmer of colour appeared ahead. Relieved, he kicked forward in a fast crawl-beat—then came to a halt and stared through the face-mask glass in frozen disbelief.

What he'd found was an apparently intact motor sailer which had settled on her side among the weed, her tiny lug-sail still tugging gently at the mast as it trapped some undersea current.

The nameplate at her stern said she was the *Emerald*. That meant nothing in itself, but every line of the little craft was identical to the motor sailer he'd last seen taking Roddy Fraser and his bride from Port MacFarlane on the start of their honeymoon trip.

Kicking forward again, Carrick reached the cockpit. The engine controls were shut off and beyond them the cabin door lay open, inviting him into a dark, green gloom. Grimly, he judged its width then wriggled through, hampered by the bulk of the air tanks on his back.

A large dogfish and several smaller shapes fled as he entered, terrified by this new arrival and the bubbles gouting from the scuba's exhaust valve. Sodden food packages and other debris drifted around him, he pushed a floating cushion aside—and then knew a moment of heart-jerking horror as a grinning human face appeared in the green murk a bare arm's length ahead.

Slack-jawed, gap-toothed, a thin halo of hair waving in the disturbed water, Francie MacPhee was anchored by a heavy fire-bar tied around his ankles. So he floated almost upright, fully clothed. And fish had already begun nibbling at his face.

Drifting back, Carrick collided with the cushion again. Half-turning to shove it away, he saw another figure, tensed, then relaxed again realising it was his own reflection in a long cupboard mirror.

Fighting down repugnance, he eased his way round Francie MacPhee's body and checked the rest of the cabin area. All its fitments were intact, but there was still something strange. Two people on a honeymoon cruise had to have luggage and clothes, however basic. But all he could locate was a set of old oilskins still attached to a bulkhead hook.

The way the little motor sailer lay, her deck was to his right. Turning his body, edging up to where one of the centre deck-boards was missing, he reached shoulder-deep into the gap, already anticipating what he'd find.

His fingers met the main sea-cock tap. It was fully open. The *Emerald* had been deliberately sunk.

Pushing himself away, Carrick finned for the cabin door again. His air tanks brushed Francie MacPhee's body and left it swaying as he reached the open cockpit then began rising up towards the light.

．　　　．　　　．　　　．　　　．

Carrick surfaced some twenty yards from the packboat and Clapper Bell quickly paddled over then helped him aboard. Shoving back his face-mask, Carrick stripped the air tanks from his back in silence. But the look on his face was enough for Bell.

"What the hell did you find down there?" he demanded sharply.

Carrick told him, and the bo'sun whistled thinly between his teeth.

"We'd better radio the Old Man," was his gruff verdict.

"Maybe." Carrick glanced at the radio pack, then slowly, almost bitterly, shook his head. "No, we'll go round and take a look at the landing stage first, Clapper. Then we'll have a better idea how things are."

Surprised, Bell shrugged a puzzled acceptance.

"Just don't expect any friendly welcome," he warned grimly.

They used the paddles only, keeping the little packboat as close under the cliffs as they dared, having to work hard to avoid being swept in against their jagged base by the long, creaming swell. At last, a swirling current swung them out as they passed a finger of rock—then they hastily backed water again and retreated into its shelter.

The landing stage lay about two hundred yards ahead with the *Razorbill* moored beside it. But the fishing boat wasn't alone. The white bulk of the *San Helena* lay another fifty or so yards off shore. But what mattered even more was the little group of people standing on the landing stage, where the *San Helena's* speedboat also tossed on a mooring line.

Dan Fraser was at home and had company. The others with him were Jimsy MacLean, Tara Grant and Frank Farrell and whatever had been happening, they seemed to be saying good-byes.

Another swell, heavier than most, came in against the packboat and took it broadside. For the next few moments Carrick and Clapper Bell fought to prevent being capsized as the packboat slammed against the rock and just managed to paddle clear before the next swell came in.

It was smaller than the last and they rode it easily. As it passed, Carrick glanced round. Clapper Bell was cursing silently, staring at where their radio had been, then he met Carrick's gaze almost miserably.

"The damned thing went over, sir. If I'd lashed it down—"

"Forget it," said Carrick bluntly. The loss came as almost welcome, settling his mind on what to do next.

They stayed in the doubtful shelter of the rock, pitching on the waves, while Tara and Farrell clambered down into the speedboat. Dan Fraser cast off the mooring line as the engine fired, and the boat quickly bounced its way out to the *San Helena*. In a matter of minutes Tara and Farrell had been helped aboard by the motor yacht's crew, the speedboat had been hoisted on the stern davits, and the *San Helena* had begun to pull away, heading north.

On the landing stage, Jimsy MacLean and Dan Fraser stood watching while the white hull quickly receded. Then they turned and went ashore, vanishing among the rocks.

"Let's go," said Carrick quietly, shifting the grip on his paddle. "Front door style, Clapper."

The Glasgow-Irishman nodded wryly. "Maybe we can ask to borrow his radio."

They paddled the remaining distance, calmly tied the packboat to the landing stage, and walked along the wooden planking to the shore. On the way they passed the *Razorbill*, which seemed deserted, and from the shore they turned towards the lobster pool. But as they trudged over the coarse shingle an all too familiar double hammer click reached their ears and they froze simultaneously.

"Just wait right there," said a nervously determined voice.

One of the fishing boat's crew emerged from the boulders just ahead. The double-barrelled shotgun in his hands was pointed squarely in their direction.

"Point that thing somewhere else, pal," said Clapper Bell almost wearily. "You know who we are."

"I know." The man moistened his lips uneasily. "Makes no difference." He raised his voice. "Dan—Dan Fraser. Over here."

There was a quick enough response. Fraser hurried into sight from the direction of the storage pool with Jimsy MacLean and a couple more of the *Razorbill*'s crew close behind.

"What the hell . . . ?" exploded Fraser, stopping short, taking in the scuba suits with eyes which were narrowed and angry. "Like to tell me what you're doing here, Carrick?"

"Looking for things—and finding them," said Carrick shortly. He thumbed towards the man with the shotgun. "Tell him to get rid of that."

"There's no hurry." Tight-lipped, Fraser almost automatically brushed his long hair back with one hand and exchanged a quick glance with Jimsy MacLean. The two fishermen with them didn't try to hide their hostility. "Looking and finding, Carrick—meaning what?"

"Get rid of that shotgun first," said Carrick softly.

Fraser glared and said nothing. But with a low growl, Clapper Bell strode forward, ignoring the rest, heading straight for the man with the shotgun. The man's eyes widened, his mouth shaped a threat—then the bo'sun had wrenched the shotgun from his hands. Almost contemptuously Bell shoved the man back, broke the gun open, flipped out its shells, and hurled shells and shotgun far among the rocks. Then he turned and faced the other fishermen, hands hanging dangerously loose at his sides.

"Is anyone else here a fightin' man?" he asked disgustedly.

There was a long, pregnant silence but nobody moved. Finally, Dan Fraser swore under his breath. He signalled the other fishermen away and they vanished back among the rocks, leaving him standing with Jimsy MacLean.

"I asked what you found, Carrick," he said again, hoarsely.

Carrick shrugged and glanced at the older man. Jimsy Mac-

Lean, dressed in worn tweeds had a tired, almost disinterested expression on his face. His one good eye met Carrick's gaze then switched away unemotionally.

"What about you, Captain?" asked Carrick softly, with a sudden understanding. "Maybe what I found matters more to you than Fraser." He paused, waiting while the man's head turned slowly again. "Where's that girl of yours, Jimsy? Do you know?"

Jimsy MacLean's mouth fell open and he looked stunned. Beside him, Dan Fraser muttered a quick caution then swing on Carrick.

"If this is some cheap trick—" he began.

"A trick?" Carrick shook his head. "Fraser, right now I don't give a damn how many rafts of lobsters you've hidden away. I don't give a damn how or why you did it—all I'm interested in is your brother and Mhari. Do you know where they are?"

Fraser swallowed and glanced helplessly at MacLean and it was MacLean who answered, his voice hoarse.

"If you know something, Carrick, for God's sake tell us."

"I know where their boat is," answered Carrick and saw their disbelief. "I can take you to it—but it's a diving job." Then, as MacLean's face drained of colour, he added swiftly, "They weren't on it, Jimsy. They were taken off first."

"You're sure?" asked MacLean desperately.

"That's how it looks," nodded Carrick.

"And you'll take us there?" asked Dan Fraser, chewing his lip. "Carrick, if you're right—"

"I'll take you there," said Carrick curtly. "Then afterwards I'm going to have some straight talk from both of you. Straight talk before it's too late."

Fraser sighed and nodded. "I'll need a loan of an aqualung. We've two sets on the *Razorbill* but—well, the air bottles are on re-charge."

"You've been busy," agreed Carrick dryly. "Come on."

Fraser and MacLean followed them back to the landing stage where Fraser boarded the fishing boat, to emerge minutes later clad in diving rubbers. Then all four men clambered down into

140

the packboat and Clapper Bell took her away with the outboard roaring.

Under power, returning to the south end of the island was a short, bouncing ride. They located the spot beneath the cliffs where Carrick had dived then, with the outboard throttled back until it was just preventing them from drifting, Carrick thumbed over the side.

"See for yourself, Fraser," he invited. "And take a look in the cabin. Take a particular look in the cabin."

Dan Fraser glanced at him sharply, but Carrick's lips were a tight line. Shrugging, the fisherman pulled on one of the aqualung sets, drew down his face-mask, and went over the side. He vanished down, a thin trail of bubbles marking his progress.

Behind the black eye-patch, Jimsy MacLean's face stayed pale and strained. But he said nothing, taking the cigarette Clapper Bell offered and smoking it in silence.

The minutes dragged past then, at last, Dan Fraser's head surfaced a few yards from the packboat. He swam over, they helped him aboard, and once he'd stripped off the aqualung he sat staring at Carrick for a moment, the water still dripping from his suit.

"You bastard," he said softly. "You said look in the cabin—"

"The way I did," Carrick told him bleakly. "That's part of it now."

"I know." Sighing, Fraser brushed the hair away from his eyes and faced Jimsy MacLean, who had been waiting as if carved from stone.

"The boat's down there, Jimsy," said Fraser wearily. "She was scuttled all right—and a couple of suitcases I put aboard for them are gone."

MacLean's face twitched but he kept the rest of his reaction to a nod.

"What else?" he asked in a beaten voice.

"Francie MacPhee's down there, weighed down with a hunk of iron." Dan Fraser slammed the side of the packboat with a despairing fist. "What a bloody mess—what a bloody awful mess."

"Can we get away from here?" asked Jimsy MacLean.

Carrick nodded. Opening up the throttle, Clapper Bell started the packboat creaming back towards the landing stage.

. . . . .

"Now," said Webb Carrick ten minutes later. "Who has them, Jimsy?"

They were in the fo'c'sle cabin of the *Razorbill*, the same cabin where only four days before he'd met the two Fraser brothers and taken part in that cheerfully drunken stag party which was to have launched Roddy Fraser into wedded bliss. It seemed cold and damp and empty now, rocking slowly as the waves heaved against the hull, an occasional creak and thump coming between as the fishing boat's fenders nudged the landing stage.

Jimsy MacLean was at one side of the cabin table. Carrick was sitting opposite, while Clapper Bell sprawled back on a bunk with a grim interest on his rugged face and Dan Fraser busied himself pouring whisky into four glasses.

"Who has them, Jimsy?" asked Carrick again.

"We don't know," said MacLean flatly. "Some gang of maniacs, somewhere—"

"The same people who sent those notes?"

MacLean's mouth sagged briefly in surprise, then he nodded.

"And the fire-bomb too, right?" Carrick didn't wait for an answer. "Jimsy, I've heard what was supposed to happen when you salvaged that tanker—the captain couldn't remember slipping and falling. Could that be the link?"

"No." It came bitterly, angrily. "That was a put-up job, Carrick. His owners were trying to save themselves some money. But it happened the way I said. I had witnesses, plenty of them—"

"Including Francie MacPhee," said Carrick unemotionally.

"Yes." MacLean's shoulders sagged at the reminder. "There was a full inquiry, Carrick. The other story was thrown out— that's why, when this started up, it didn't make sense."

"But he's the kind of stubborn old devil who goes it alone," growled Dan Fraser. He set down filled glasses in front of them, handed one to Clapper Bell, and took a quick gulp from his own. "Tell them the rest, Jimsy, it's short enough."

"Roddy and Mhari sailed off that night—you saw them go," said MacLean, nursing his glass between visibly shaking fingers. "Next morning, early on, I had a telephone call. A voice I'd heard before about the tanker business—there were 'phone calls as well as the notes. He said they had Roddy and Mhari. If I wanted proof, I was to go down to the beach near the harbour. He told me where to look."

He reached slowly into a pocket then placed a gold wedding ring on the table.

"That's what I found, inside a tobacco tin." His voice fought to remain steady. "It's Mhari's—the initials inside, everything about it."

"I'll vouch for that," said Dan Fraser softly. "I was their best man, remember?"

Carrick started to reach for the ring, then left it there and asked simply, "What happened next?"

"More messages, more proof—a knife of Roddy's, a lock of Mhari's hair." MacLean drew a long, shaky breath, a man still living in a nightmare. "They want three-quarters of what I got for the tanker salvage, Carrick—£75,000 by the end of the week."

From the bunk, Clapper Bell gave a long, appreciative whistle.

"Can you do it?" he asked bluntly.

"He can now," said Dan Fraser thinly. "He's selling this island to Frank Farrell."

"Farrell?" Carrick blinked. "He told me he didn't want to know about Horsehead Island."

"He talked about it once, vaguely—when I didn't want to sell," said MacLean. "He wasn't doing much more than being polite. But—" he shrugged "—Tara thought he might be interested if the price was right. I tried, and he was."

Carrick frowned. "How much does Tara know?"

"Just that I'm short of cash. I've only told Dan the real story—no-one else."

"And there's nothing I can do when money is involved," admitted Fraser bitterly. "Even the *Razorbill* is in Roddy's name."

"When does the sale go through?" demanded Carrick.

"We'll sign the papers tomorrow. Sixty thousand pounds, cash

143

—I can raise the other fifteen thousand all right." MacLean barely moistened his lips with the whisky. "Then I pay them, Carrick. Don't try to interfere—I can't risk it."

There was a silence in the cabin for a moment, broken only by the fishing boat's creaking and bumping. Then, his face a puzzled frown, Clapper Bell hoisted himself forward on the bunk.

"But what the devil can even a chancer like Farrell do wi' an ugly chunk of rock like this?" he demanded.

"That's his affair," said MacLean wearily. "I don't care. There are folk who'll buy anything, I suppose—I had my own reasons, but even Dirk Peters had second thoughts after he sold to me." He grimaced at the memory. "Peters wanted to cancel the sale, even offered me a drop of compensation for my trouble when I said I wasn't cancelling."

Carrick scraped a slow hand across his chin, frowning. In his mind, he was struggling with several flimsy possibilities, few of them making separate sense yet all somehow leading towards a pattern which still had no basic reason.

"I want to hear about Halley Bay," he said suddenly.

"That?" Dan Fraser grunted irately. "Who the hell would bother about a few lobsters now? Anyway—"

"I said Halley Bay," snapped Carrick, cutting him short. "Francie MacPhee was there—and here's two more items for the list, Fraser. What about that fisherman, Christie? Right now the County police think he was murdered, with your brother the nearest thing they've got to a suspect." He ignored Fraser's startled protest. "I said two items. Do you imagine *Marlin* went on that reef by accident?"

The complete bewilderment on Fraser's face was its own answer and justified Carrick going on.

"Our steering gear was sabotaged," he said bluntly, then went on in a cold, factual voice, helping his own thoughts in the process. "Fit it together. Christie dies—almost certainly because he saw who sabotaged *Marlin*. But *Marlin* was sabotaged because she had to be unable to sail the night of the Halley Bay raid—the night that was also when Roddy and Mhari were grabbed."

Fraser swallowed hard. "There's no connection, Carrick. Not between Halley Bay and the rest—my word on it."

"You're saying it was just coincidence?" asked Carrick bleakly. Fraser nodded.

"Tell him what you told me," urged Jimsy MacLean. Then, as Fraser hesitated doubtfully, a harsh urgency entered the older man's voice. "Tell him, damn you, or I will."

"Suppose I help?" Carrick suggested with a deceptive mildness. "Two brothers have everything going for them—including a storage pool crammed with lobsters. Then they find they've an outbreak of Red Tail on their hands, an outbreak they know will be an epidemic within days. I'd call that a disaster, right?"

Fraser stared at him, then managed a nod.

"Stage one," mused Carrick. "Stage two—well, we'll say someone had a notion how to get new stock. A clever, thieving notion. When the wedding celebrations are in full swing nobody will notice if a certain fishing boat's crew slip away—and they know the party will go on for hours, that they'll be able to reappear and never have been missed. So Francie MacPhee gets knocked on the head and those rafts vanish."

"Old Francie wasn't knocked," protested Fraser, then caution took over. "I'll play it your way, Carrick. I'll guess he was blind drunk when they got there. Out cold, where he'd fallen, with the empty bottle still in his hand. If there was a bump on his head, he got it when he fell. Maybe somebody thought it was a kindness to tie him up."

"You gave him a bottle o' that home-made dynamite," grunted Clapper Bell. "He told us."

"But nobody from this boat went near *Marlin*," grated Fraser. He turned appealingly to Carrick. "Hell, Roddy didn't even spot the Red Tail outbreak—and I didn't tell him. I wanted my wee brother to sail out of here without any worries."

"Those lobster rafts still vanished," said Carrick softly. He considered the fisherman bleakly. "Where would you try looking for them?"

"You don't give up, do you?" asked Fraser thickly. "There's a

145

sea-cave on the west side here. You could sail past the spot a dozen times and never find it."

"It can wait." Carrick turned to Jimsy MacLean, understanding the expression of near-contempt on the older man's face. "I had to know, Jimsy—and it's all relevant to finding that girl of yours."

"Finding?" MacLean gave a noise like a groan. "Carrick, I told you—"

"Two murders already, Jimsy—Christie and MacPhee," reminded Carrick dispassionately. "You tell me where there's most risk." He saw it sink home. "So let's try and put another part together. When did Peters want this island back, and why?"

"About a month after he sold—he just said he'd changed his mind." MacLean sucked his cheeks, remembering. "I said no, and that was that—people usually know when I mean something."

"True," murmured Carrick. "Where was Mhari then?"

"In London, working in that television place—"

"And Peters turned up there with Farrell not long afterwards," reminded Carrick. "But the threats didn't begin till later."

MacLean nodded. "Just after Mhari became engaged."

"Hold on." Speculation took over from puzzlement in Dan Fraser's attitude. "Carrick, are you hinting that—"

"I'm asking, not hinting," said Carrick shortly. "Jimsy, you went to Halley Bay and saw Francie MacPhee. Why?"

"The same reason I'd seen him a couple of times before. Because he was with me on the tanker salvage and I thought—well, I thought maybe he knew what was behind it all. He still swore he didn't, but—"

"But he might have, eh?" suggested Clapper Bell dispassionately. "Talked to somebody about it all for the price o' a bottle?"

MacLean nodded.

"Think back to last night," said Carrick quietly. "You were leaving the house with a brief-case when I arrived. Why?"

"They—they'd 'phoned again, wanting my answer." MacLean's voice was strained and shaky again. "I said I was trying to raise the money. Then—well, I went down to the harbour, to see Farrell. He wasn't on the *San Helena*, but their skipper went up the village and found Dirk Peters. He said Farrell was over in Tobermory and wouldn't be driving back till late on. I left a message and—and Farrell came up to the house this morning."

Carrick nodded. It meant it could have been Farrell and two of the *San Helena* crew who had jumped him at Halley Bay. Which could also mean something more—something which left him with a sick feeling at how he might have been fooled.

"One last thing, Jimsy," he said in a flat voice. "Where did you get the idea to sell the island?"

"It was the obvious thing, wasn't it?" answered MacLean almost irritably. "When I bought the island, I had a fancy notion I was recapturing the family heritage—thinking of all those dead generations of MacLeans and what a great hero I was." He touched the black eye-patch. "Carrick, I lost this eye being another kind of hero by some folk's reckoning, in a wartime caper. But I'd give the other eye—and anything else I have—to get Mhari back. And that new husband of hers. I like the boy."

"But did anyone suggest selling the island?" persisted Carrick.

"Yes—yes, I suppose—" MacLean caught the significance and a new shock showed on his face "—they did, those people. In a couple of the 'phone calls I had before the wedding. They said if I could afford to buy Horsehead Island I could afford to sell it again to pay up."

Dan Fraser laid both hands flat on the table with a demanding thud.

"Carrick, let's get this straight," he said urgently. "Your bet is Farrell and Peters, right?"

"Can either of them use scuba gear?" asked Carrick.

"Peters can—I've seen him," nodded Fraser. "Why?"

"Francie MacPhee," grunted Clapper Bell. "You don't think he was on that boat when it was scuttled, do you? And *Marlin*'s steering was flaked up by someone who maybe got aboard that way."

"Well?" persisted Fraser.

"Farrell and Peters," agreed Carrick. "Don't ask me why they want this rockpile—but they must." He rose and went over to the cabin's tiny porthole, looking thoughtfully out at the sea. Time had slipped past. In little more than an hour it would be dusk. "It would help if we knew where that damned *San Helena* was going."

"But we do," said Fraser excitedly. "That's why Tara's with them, for the trip. Peters is going a cruise trip up the coast to the north end of Mull, tourist style. Then they're sailing across to the Treshnish Isles, so Tara can see the seals at dawn or some bloody thing like that. Farrell told me they'd land on Sgeir Fionn Isle —there's a wartime army installation on Sgeir Fionn, abandoned but still in reasonable shape, if they want to spend the night ashore."

"That's right." Jimsy MacLean moistened his lips. "Tara made a joke about it all—safety in numbers, she said." He sighed. "It's maybe my fault she went. Life at Ard-Tulach hasn't been easy the last couple of days, the way I've been going around."

Carrick barely heard him. He was thinking of the Treshnishes, a tight scatter of mostly barren, totally uninhabited islets seldom visited by anyone.

MacLean suddenly shot upright from the table, with the same idea.

"They could be there, on Sgeir Fionn. If we could get there first—"

"On what?" asked Dan Fraser bleakly. "Can you magic back that helicopter, Carrick?"

"Not in time," admitted Carrick. "And you can forget *Marlin* —she's in no state for it."

"And this boat hasn't any kind of speed," said Fraser grimly. "So what's left?"

"The packboat," declared Clapper Bell, grinning at them. "Hell, she could beat that sugar-iced monstrosity they're on any day. All she needs is refuelling—"

"I can cope with that." Fraser was suddenly hopeful. "Anything else?"

Bell nodded. "We should radio the Old Man first. Right, sir?"

"No radio," said Carrick flatly. The fishing frequency was about as private as shouting across a crowded room and *Marlin's* emergency frequencies were too low down the waveband for the kind of equipment carried by boats like the *Razorbill*. "No, that's your job, Jimsy. Fraser's crew can sail you over to Port MacFarlane. Get hold of Captain Shannon, tell him what we're doing, and he'll get the rest moving."

"I should be with you," protested MacLean furiously. "My girl—"

"Your girl is maybe needing all the help she can get," said Carrick brutally. "Peters has a house on Mull, right? We want that checked too, and fast."

Tight-lipped, MacLean shrugged and nodded.

"But we've room for one more on the packboat," added Carrick thoughtfully, glancing at Dan Fraser. "If he was a man who really knows the Treshnishes."

"I know every rock out there by its first name," said Fraser happily, and finished his drink at a gulp. "I'm ready."

CHAPTER EIGHT

Five minutes later both boats had left the landing stage at Horsehead Island. The *Razorbill*'s crew, told enough by Dan Fraser to send them on their way with Jimsy MacLean aboard and a wry uncertainty on their faces, turned her blunt nose towards Mull and set off for Port MacFarlane. The packboat began a searing, full-throttle northerly course towards the distant Treshnish Isles.

Clapper Bell was in his usual place at the packboat's tiller. In front of him, Webb Carrick and Dan Fraser huddled down while the little inflatable bounced and pitched over the long Atlantic swells with her bow high out of the water and the freshening westerly wind whipping drenching curtains of spray over her length from each wave-top.

Jammed between the packboat's rubberised hull and the two aqualung outfits, Carrick avoided any thought of planning for what lay ahead. For the moment, it was enough that they were on their way. He was gambling and he knew it.

But every instinct told him he had to be right. And the Treshnish Isles made total sense as the place where Roddy Fraser and his bride might be held captive.

A cluster of grassy islands, barren islets and high, toothed rocks, they stretched south-west to north-east in a narrow, five-mile oval off the northerly tip of Mull. From Bac Beg and the Dutchman's Cap at the south-west to the precipitous, almost inaccessible Cairn na Burgh Beg at the north-east extremity, they encompassed a nightmare stretch of water even by Hebridean standards.

A nightmare which was laced by snaking channels through unexpected shallows, with a middle-ground maze of fanged rocks and half-tide reefs. In mid-summer and fine weather, adventurous yachtsmen treated the Treshnishes as a playground. But most of the year they stayed what they were—sullen, dangerous, deserted, guarded on the east by a strong ebb tide and on the south-west by more foul ground.

Sgeir Fionn was an island in the thickest part of the long oval, in the middle-ground maze. Normally, Carrick would not have wanted to go anywhere near it in any size of craft.

But if the *San Helena* was heading there he had no choice. He glanced at Dan Fraser, who stirred and grinned at him as another curtain of spray drenched over them.

Fraser was another part of his gamble, as much a part as sending Jimsy MacLean off to Port MacFarlane. He needed the long-haired, thin-faced fisherman—but there was still a difference between need and total trust.

The packboat raced on. As the sun began to set they passed the tall, fantastically columnated cliffs of Staffa, keeping the island well to starboard yet still able to see the long, black shadow which marked the seventy-foot-high entrance to Fingal's Cave.

Staffa had inspired music which would live for ever. But to Carrick, glimpsing it each time the inflatable rode high on a swell, it was a warning there was still a long way to go.

In fact, the sky was edging grey with the first hints of dusk when the Treshnish group showed ahead. Hauling himself up, Dan Fraser peered through salt-rimmed eyes at the land shaping on their port bow then crouched down and shouted in Carrick's ear above the outboard's rasping bellow.

"That's the south end of Lunga—we're coming in just about right." He paused hopefully. "I'll take over from your bo'sun anytime."

Carrick left that till the high, terraced shore of Lunga was clearly visible. Then he signalled and Fraser and Bell changed position. Settled in, Fraser took a minute or two to get the feel of the outboard then leaned forward.

"The quick way?" he shouted.

Carrick nodded. They veered to starboard and seemed to be heading straight for a smaller island which had appeared. But Fraser skirted it and as they rounded a final point Carrick had his first glimpse of what lay in front of them in the deepening grey. He felt his stomach tighten and a simultaneous curse from Clapper Bell told him the feeling was shared.

The packboat was pointed straight for an apparently endless cauldron of boiling, broken waves, swirling eddies and sharp-toothed rocks which were clouded in spray. If there was any safe way through, he couldn't see even a sign of it.

"I said a quick way," bellowed Fraser encouragingly, sensing their reaction. "I didn't say it was easy—but we'll get there. Just hang on an' don't worry."

Huddling lower, Carrick envied the fisherman his confidence. Then he only had time for a deep breath before they were committed, whitewater style.

Bucking and twisting, the inflatable protested and shuddered beneath them as it entered the full terror of the barrier's cauldron. Within seconds, foam-tipped walls of green water had begun smashing down on them or clawing and hammering at the rubberised hull while Fraser fought against each succeeding peril. Hunched at the tiller in total concentration, long hair clinging soaked to his head, he kept his eyes ahead and his teeth tight clenched while he forced the little boat to obey him.

New sounds rose above the thunder of the waves and the bellow of the outboard—the scream of the propeller each time their stern was heaved bodily and the blades bit empty air, the awesome, drum-like booming as trapped breakers smashed their anger against time-worn rock. All around, reef rock appeared and vanished and appeared again in the turmoil of frothing, maddened water.

Clinging to a life-line, drenching and drenched again, Carrick had a glimpse of Clapper Bell's lips moving soundlessly. The tortured sound of the outboard seemed like their heartbeat, one falter enough for disaster.

Then, almost as suddenly as it had begun, it was over. The packboat was in a rapidly widening channel leading into a broad stretch of clear water where the swell was steady and regular and, by comparison, almost placid. A new pattern of islands stretched ahead in the dusk and Dan Fraser was throttling back, grinning at them.

"There's the one we want," he said assuredly, pointing to one of the largest islands. "That's Sgeir Fionn."

Easing up, water trickling down his scuba rubbers, Carrick looked, saw for himself, and nodded. Sgeir Fionn had breakers speckling white off its shore but after what they'd come through it seemed almost welcoming.

"Where would you anchor something the size of the *San Helena?*" he asked.

"There's a small bay on the west side—it dries out partly at low tide, but it's safe enough." Fraser waited, his face becoming more serious.

"We'll try it. But go in easy—and quietly," said Carrick.

Nodding, Fraser settled the packboat on its new course and throttled back even more till the engine note was not much more than a murmur easily lost among the waves. Fumbling in a suit pocket, Clapper Bell miraculously produced dry cigarettes and matches from a small tin. He lit three cigarettes carefully and passed them one each. Then, drawing deep on the smoke, he looked back at where they'd been and shook his head slowly.

"Never do that to me again," he said solemnly. "Hell, I'd rather walk."

Keeping a few hundred yards out, they crept round the south tip of Sgeir Fionn and began moving up its west shore. Already, the deepening dusk was beginning to obscure all but the island's main features and a line of white breakers ahead was the first warning of a low headland shielding the bay which was Fraser's goal.

They passed it, the stretch of sheltered water behind it appeared —and Carrick fought down a groan. Despite what they'd come through, they'd lost. The *San Helena* was anchored there, about two hundred yards out. Light shone from her upper deck and other pinpricks of light showed ashore.

"Well, we tried," said Dan Fraser bleakly, staring at the lights. "But what the hell do we do now?"

"Ease back on that throttle." Carrick waited till the packboat was almost stationary, with little more than steering way.

"Those lights ashore, Dan—you said there was an old army installation."

"That's it," nodded Fraser. "A place like a small fort which is still intact. There are some huts too, but they're pretty much in ruins."

Carrick pondered. The *San Helena* had swung bow-on to her anchor but was still pitching in the kind of way which would be uncomfortable for anyone aboard. That left the likelihood that most of her people were ashore—a likelihood that was worth some risk.

"We'll drift in, then paddle up towards her stern. But not yet." He gauged the gathering darkness and decided another fifteen minutes should be enough to completely cloak their approach. "When we get there, you stay with the packboat. Understand?"

Fraser scowled but nodded.

"Just don't leave me out later," he said grimly. "I've the biggest stake in this lot, Carrick—remember that."

. . . . . .

The moon was out but partly obscured by cloud when the packboat drifted in. A low, grey shadow on the sea, she passed the *San Helena* then turned as her paddles set to work.

Nothing moved on the motor yacht's deck as they came in under her stern, though the radar scanner above her superstructure was turning steadily. The packboat bumped lightly, came in again, then, as the two craft rose and fell together, Carrick and Clapper Bell jumped for the low transom rail. They clung for a moment as the motor yacht gave a deep curtsy to another swell then swung themselves aboard. From the packboat, Fraser threw a light line and they secured it to a deck stanchion, signalled everything was all right, then padded forward.

The lights on the *San Helena* came from a combined radio and navigation room below her cockpit bridge and for'ard of the main passenger accommodation. Their black rubber suits merging into the night, Carrick and Bell peered through a window.

Two of the motor yacht's crew lounged inside. One was reading a magazine and the second man was dozing but their purpose was clear—the glow of a radar screen beside the man with the magazine and the thin crackle of a radio receiver which, even as they eased back again, came to life with a brief exchange of messages between two distant fishing boats.

"They don't take chances," muttered Clapper Bell once they'd retired a few paces. "What's the bettin' on a ship to shore radio link on top o' that?"

The same thought had been in Carrick's mind and held him back from his first notion to rush the crewmen. He signalled Bell to follow and led the way aft until he reached a companionway door which led into the passenger accommodation. It was unlocked and he turned to the bo'sun with a purposeful grin.

"Keep an eye on things here, Clapper—but I don't want trouble. If these two get restless, let me know straight off."

Nodding, Bell patted the sheathed diving knife at his hip then took up position in the nearest patch of shadow.

The layout of the passenger area like a blueprint in his mind, Carrick went in, closed the door gently behind him, and made his way along the narrow, wood-panelled companionway. There was enough moonlight coming through the superstructure windows to let him identify the doors of the guest cabins and he ignored them, heading for the owner's cabin, which Dirk Peters used. Reaching it, he went in and carefully drew the curtains before feeling his way back across the darkness to the bed and switching on a small reading lamp.

Then he began searching quickly and carefully. The wardrobe and lockers held little but clothing and the only papers he found related to the *San Helena*. But as he was on the point of giving up he spotted a tightly rolled chart on a shelf above some books.

Bringing the chart down, he spread it out on the bed and saw it was a standard Admiralty sheet for the Western Isles. But what puzzled and fascinated him was the way someone had sprinkled it with inked markings and lines—all radiating from Horsehead Island. Soundings were circled, and arrows pointed to shoal areas. But the lines, marked in red ink, were even more puzzling.

One came from a question-marked beginning in the open Atlantic, snaked a way through the Outer Isles which only the smallest of coasters could have followed, then came across the

Minch to Horsehead Island. Then a double line from the island followed the main deep-water track south while a single, dotted line curved round Mull to the mainland and ended in another question mark.

Carrick stared at the chart for a minute longer, part of its sense gradually percolating through.

Horsehead Island sat on the edge of a uniquely clear deep-water channel from the open Atlantic to the south. Seldom less than a mile broad and fifty fathoms deep, it was a channel splendidly sheltered from the worst of storms by the Outer Isles. Why that mattered and the significance of the other lines was a separate mystery.

But an odd notion was stirring in his mind as he rolled the chart tight again and replaced it. A notion he needed time to think about.

Switching out the light and opening the curtains again, he left the cabin, went back along the companionway, and emerged on deck again to join Clapper Bell.

Quietly, they went back to the stern. Unhitching the packboat's line, they followed it down into the water and moments later Dan Fraser was helping them back aboard the little inflatable.

"Well?" asked Fraser in an eager whisper as they drifted away. "Any luck?"

"Two men left on radio and radar watch," Carrick told him softly. "We took a look around, but that's all."

"Hell." Fraser's face fell. "You're sure?"

Carrick nodded, conscious that Clapper Bell was eyeing him oddly. But it was no time to start theorising or mentioning the chart. Reaching for one of the paddles, he grinned encouragingly at Fraser.

"We'll try the island now. And this time, Clapper stays with the packboat. All right?"

"Fine." Fraser gave a satisfied grunt and lifted the other paddle.

.   .   .   .

They beached the packboat about five hundred yards north of the twinkling lights on shore, hauled the inflatable up over the sand, and left it hidden behind the cover of some rocks. Then

Carrick and Fraser set off along the shore-line towards the lights, leaving Clapper Bell glumly resigned to being sentry again.

Most of the way, gorse and rock provided plenty of cover. But they paused at the edge of a cleared area, looking at the building now in front of them. Seen close up, the one-time army installation looked like plenty of other World War Two military outposts left scattered around the islands. A single-storey brick structure about the size of a large house, it was topped by an observation tower—though the tower's windows were smashed and a single shutter, all that remained, hung loose and ready to fall. Lights showed behind three of the ground-floor windows and smoke from a driftwood fire scented the cool night air.

They were about to go nearer when a door swung open and a man stepped out.

Carrick heard a gasp come from Fraser then they both froze. The man was one of the *San Helena's* crew but his mission was peaceful enough. Framed in the lighted doorway, he walked forward a few paces then solemnly dumped a pail of garbage. He went back with the emptied pail, the door closed, and Carrick breathed again.

"He was lucky, that one," muttered Dan Fraser in an odd voice.

For the first time, Carrick saw the gun in his hand, a heavy Webley automatic pistol with the safety catch still on. Fraser grinned uneasily at his scrutiny.

"I—uh—Jimsy MacLean gave me it to bring along," he explained with a shrug. "I had it under my suit. It kind of makes sense, doesn't it?"

"Just remember we didn't come here to start a war," murmured Carrick. "What's round the back of this place?"

"Only those old huts I told you about." Fraser tucked the gun away with some reluctance. "Most of them don't have as much as a roof."

"Then we'll forget them and get in closer." Carrick gauged the distance across the clearing. "From now on, think like you're walking on eggs."

The moon came out from behind a cloudbank exactly as they were halfway over. But they reached the wall of the building, hugged the cold brickwork and heard a murmur of voices from somewhere near. Easing along to the nearest of the lighted windows, Carrick looked in through a chink in the sacking which served as a crude curtain.

The crewman who had emptied the bucket was there, piling more driftwood on a fire blazing in a hearth, while Frank Farrell leaned against a doorway talking to him. It was impossible to make out what Farrell was saying but the man at the fire looked up, answered, and Farrell laughed then went away.

Drawing back, Carrick returned to Dan Fraser.

"Looks like they could all be inside," he said softly. "Stay here and I'll work my way round."

Moistening his lips, Fraser nodded. His hand was back in his opened scuba suit, resting on the butt of the Webley, as Carrick set off.

Rubbish littered the ground at the rear of the building and Carrick had to go carefully. One lighted room held some bedrolls spread on the concrete floor, but was deserted. The next few windows were in darkness then he stopped at one, where the frame had gone and all that remained was a gaping hole. Pulling himself up on the ledge, Carrick swung a leg over, ready to climb in.

A hoarse, warning shout from where he'd left Fraser stopped him. The shout was followed by the bark of a gun, a sharper crack from a different weapon and a curse of pain . . . then a powerful torch flared in the night and the beam pinned him where he was.

"Stay just like that," snapped Dirk Peters' voice from behind the light. "Don't try anything fancy unless you want a hole in the head. Now come down from there—slowly."

Tight-lipped, Carrick obeyed while shouts came from the army building Peters answered reassuringly. Then two figures came towards him along the side of the wall. Dan Fraser was in the lead, clutching his right arm below the shoulder. The other was Tessin, the *San Helena*'s skipper, who had an automatic in one fist and Fraser's Webley hanging negligently in the other.

"Shove them together," ordered Peters, coming forward with the torch. "Let's see what we've got."

Fraser was pushed roughly against Carrick then Peters shone the torch in their faces and swore bitterly.

"Surprised?" asked Carrick mildly.

"Move," said Peters grimly. "Into the house." The torch stayed steady on Carrick's face but his other hand rammed the muzzle of another automatic hard and painfully into Carrick's stomach. "Just do it—and don't fool about."

They were shoved on, the torch showing blood oozing between Fraser's fingers where he still clutched his bullet-torn arm. A door had opened ahead and another of the *San Helena*'s crew waited there, clutching a rifle.

"Looks like those—those eggs you talked about got broken, Carrick," managed Fraser with a wince as another shove from Tessin slammed him against the doorpost. He glanced round at Peters as they were shoved through. "Where's my brother, you lousy bamfpot?"

Stonily, Peters signalled him on. They were pushed along a short corridor then into a room which held a few sticks of broken-down furniture. Two pressure lamps threw a bright light on Frank Farrell, who stared at them as if they were particularly unwelcome ghosts. Carrick almost ignored him for the moment. Tara Grant was sitting in a chair in the corner of the room, grimy and dishevelled, her sweater torn, and the broad red mark of a blow discolouring one side of her face. She couldn't rise. Her wrists were tied to the chair behind her back. But she looked at him with something close to a dumb despair.

"These two!" Farrell licked his lips and glanced anxiously at Peters. "Any more of them, Dirk?"

"We'll find out." Peters swung towards Tessin. "Harry, check the beach. And you'd better radio the boat, Frank—hell knows how this happened."

The yacht skipper went back out towards the night, taking the other crewman with him. Still licking his lips, Farrell vanished into another room.

"Well," said Carrick wryly, looking around. "It's cosy enough, I suppose."

"It's all you'll get." Peters made a dry sound like a laugh then relaxed a little as the crewman Carrick had seen earlier busy with chores entered the room. The man had a length of thin rope and glanced at Peters, who nodded.

It took only a couple of minutes to lash their wrists behind their backs then the man went out and Peters tucked the gun away.

"Say hello to your friends, Tara," he invited acidly. "You were talkative enough before they came."

"Was I?" She looked at him bitterly then turned her head towards Carrick. "Webb, I—some of this is my fault. I'm sorry. I —" she bit her lip "—I just didn't know what I'd got into."

"We heard that too," agreed Peters. Walking over to a table, he lifted an opened bottle of beer and took a quick gulp. Then, wiping his lips on his sleeve, he considered Carrick sardonically. "You damned fool. You should have kept your nose out of this."

"I've been telling myself that," mused Carrick. He twisted a grin towards Tara. "Still, at least you've got company now. Maybe kind Mr. Peters will cut you loose long enough to fix Dan's shoulder."

"Like hell," began Peters bleakly, then stopped as Farrell came back into the room with a small walkie-talkie unit still in one hand.

"They say there's nothing on radar except what seems like a bunch of fishing boats, and they're far enough off," said Farrell with relief and forced a grin. "No radio chatter that matters either —so maybe it could be worse."

"Not much." Peters perched himself on the edge of the table. "We'll wait for Tessin."

Farrell nodded, his confidence returning. "How did you find them?"

"Luck. We were coming back from the cottage and Tessin spotted them creeping around outside here." Peters sneered in

Carrick's direction. "We'd been checking on some other guests, Carrick. No harm in admitting that now."

"That's the reason we came looking," murmured Carrick. "Dan and I had this hunch—"

"What about Roddy and Mhari?" interrupted Fraser hoarsely. The blood which had been trickling down his scuba suit was now dripping on the concrete at his feet. "If you've harmed them—"

"They're safe enough," Farrell told him laconically. "You said a hunch, Carrick—" his eyes narrowed "—what kind of hunch?"

"Just putting things together." Carrick shrugged as best he could, then baited it a little. "But when I saw that chart on the *San Helena*, I wished I'd been surer—then I'd have brought company."

A startled glance passed between Peters and Farrell.

"We were there," agreed Carrick. "Your two guard-dogs aren't the brightest. But congratulations all the same. It's been a nice squeeze play. Except for a couple of murders along the way."

"And you know about that too?" Peters said it almost sadly, then nodded. "I wondered about the scuba suits. You found the motor sailer?"

"The boat, and Francie MacPhee." Carrick heard Tara gasp and looked at her wryly. "Our friends have a motto, Tara. When in doubt, wipe out."

"Not from choice," said Farrell grimly. "Still, it solves things."

"Like Christie knowing who'd been sabotaging *Marlin* and Mac-Phee being able to talk about who'd pumped him for background on Jimsy MacLean's tanker salvage?" queried Carrick.

They ignored him as a shout came from the corridor outside. Carrick tensed, then relaxed as Tessin came into the room alone and dumped two aqualung sets on the floor.

"These were in a boat lyin' along the beach," he said shortly. "No sign of anyone else."

"Two aqualungs, and two of them." Peters said like a sigh. Coming down from the table, grinning a little, he came over and hit Carrick a hard back-handed blow across the mouth. "So you really did come free-lancing?"

"You can always wait and find out," said Carrick bleakly, tasting blood on his lips and hoping no-one else had seen the quick look of hope in Dan Fraser's eyes. As long as Clapper Bell was roaming around somewhere outside like a large and vengeful panther, their chances weren't finished. "Too bad, isn't it? There you were, nearly home and dry—Jimsy MacLean all ready to sign the deal. How much is Horsehead Island really worth, Farrell?"

"Maybe ten times what I'm paying—and even that he's handing back interest." Farrell signalled to Tessin, who went out again, then lit a cigarette and blew the smoke in Carrick's direction. "But who says it's over? We've only a new complication—you two."

Carrick shrugged. "Should I try and guess why the island is so important?"

"Why not?" Farrell grinned a little. "I'm interested in how much you're guessing."

"Well, there's that deep-water channel," mused Carrick almost reasonably. "I would take the largest ship built—if there was any good reason for that kind of ship to come this way." He wasn't finished. "Tara told me you worked for a spell in the Middle East. Which unfortunate oil company had you on its pay-roll?"

Staring at him, Farrell forgot about his cigarette for a moment. Then, slowly he nodded.

"Congratulations," he said softly, his thin face a stony mask. "Go on."

"The Hebridean field—when they start tapping that, it will make the North Sea strikes look puny. But it'll be open Atlantic." Carrick paused, but there was neither correction nor comment. "That's no place to pipe-feed a tanker, yet the cost per mile of undersea is fierce. So—Horsehead Island. Deep water, sheltered water, and a ready-made terminal point for the biggest tankers to come in and load. Plus a handy junction point for any pipeline run-off to the mainland. Your pal Peters must have felt a fool when he found out—and couldn't do a damn thing about it because he'd already sold to Jimsy MacLean."

Muttering a curse, Dirk Peters stepped forward and brought his hand up again. But Farrell stopped him with a quick headshake.

"We'll talk about it," said Farrell shortly. "Get someone in to keep an eye on them."

Peters scowled but went out and fetched the crewman with the rifle. Ordered to sit on the floor beside Tara's chair, Carrick and Fraser squatted down then the two men left, the crewman staying near the door. After a moment or two the guard yawned and leaned back against the wall, the rifle pointed casually and disinterestedly in his prisoners' direction.

"Webb." Low-voiced, almost pleading, Tara broke the silence. "I meant it. I—I didn't know about Mhari and Roddy."

"All right." Carrick looked up at her sadly. "But you knew a lot, didn't you, Tara? And you were working for them?"

She nodded. On her other side, Dan Fraser stared at them, bewildered. Carrick glanced at the crewman by the door. He was yawning again.

"Why?" he asked quietly.

"Something that happened in London." A flush crossed her bruised face. "I—well, I was a fool. Frank Farrell said he'd bail me out of it, but only if I helped."

"The kind of trouble he might have set up for you in the first place?"

"That's the way it looks now," she said wearily. "He said he had to swing this deal with Mhari's father—that it might mean pressuring him a little, though nobody would really get hurt. I was to— well, help out from the inside. Some of the notes Jimsy found— things like that."

"Including tipping Dirk Peters that I'd gone to Halley Bay that night?"

"Yes," she admitted reluctantly. "He telephoned Farrell, who was still there. Then they ripped out the 'phone wires at the hut. But—that's why I felt so sick when I saw how they'd left you. They always swore nobody would be hurt, Webb. And—and I was fool enough to believe them."

"What about Mhari and Roddy?" asked Dan Fraser in a mutter.

"They had men hidden on the boat before it sailed," she said, avoiding Fraser's gaze. "That's about all I know, Dan. Tessin, their skipper, let it slip out on our way here. Then—" she stopped and shook her head wearily.

"Who hit you?" asked Carrick.

"Farrell." She drew a deep breath. "Dan, this cottage—"

"I think I know it," grunted Fraser. "Not that it makes much odds. Unless—"

Carrick frowned him to silence. He'd been trying the ropes round his wrists, but seamen made few mistakes when it came to knots.

"Dan." He let his voice sink to a whisper. "When they come back, there's a chance they'll try to do a deal with you—you alone. Play along with it, understand? We need time."

Puzzled, Fraser nodded. "Why me?"

"Because they need you." Carrick left it there. But if he was right, the same certainly didn't apply to himself and Tara. He saw the guard frowning in their direction and raised his voice a little. "At least we know about Horsehead Island now."

"You do," said Fraser bleakly. "It still doesn't make much sense to me. This Hebridean field business—"

"The energy crunch." Seeing their guard was listening now and glad of the chance to lull his suspicions, Carrick shifted into a more comfortable position on the concrete and grimaced. "You know about that, right?"

"No more oil by the turn o' the century?" Fraser sniffed. "A lot of people say that's a load o' high grade bird manure."

"No more cheap oil," corrected Carrick. "So the oil world are going for the stuff they've ignored now. North Sea is an example —it costs millions to get those rigs and drilling platforms working, but they reckon it worth it. But as far back as forty years ago any geology student could have told you there were even bigger oil fields waiting in theory out beyond the Hebrides. Except no-one wanted to know about them."

"And now they matter, eh?" Fraser understood.

"Now they matter." Carrick thought for a moment of the fantastic battle that lay ahead for the technicians and engineers involved. Deep-water drilling far beyond the horizon of the most westerly islands, in waters where Force Ten gales were common-place. "The big boys are getting ready, the Government will start parcelling out plot allocations before long—but it's the kind of game where you look years ahead."

A rumble from Fraser told him he didn't need to spell out the rest. "So Farrell was told to go and buy an island as a tank farm terminal . . ."

"But quietly, so the price stayed reasonable," nodded Carrick. He couldn't help the wisp of a grin which crossed his face. "Imagine how Peters felt when he realised what he'd tossed away."

A guffaw came from their guard.

"You tell it real good, mister," said the man sarcastically. "But it won't help much now, eh?"

Which was true. They fell silent for a moment and before anyone could speak again Farrell and Peters came back into the room. Farrell went straight over to the walkie-talkie, which he'd left lying on the table, and spoke into it quietly for a moment. The reply which came through the earpiece seemed to satisfy him. Setting down the walkie-talkie, he nodded to Peters.

"Still just those fishing boats on the radar screen. They're nearer, but they're probably heading north."

"Anything on the radio?" demanded Peters sharply.

"Just a few skippers, gabbling to each other in Gaelic," shrugged Farrell. "God knows what they're going on about."

Carrick could imagine. Among the West Highland fleets, the old Gaelic language was as good as talking in code—unless the Fishery Protection ship listening also had a Gaelic speaker aboard.

"Right." Peters crossed over and frowned down at Dan Fraser. "Fraser, your brother and the girl are all right—we've told you that. They'll stay that way, and there could be a small slice of the profits in this for you if you play along."

"Me?" Fraser looked up at him with a deliberate dullness. "Why?"

"Because it would be—well, embarrassing if you disappeared," said Peters shortly. "Once MacLean signs over the island we'll keep our part of the deal. Your brother and the girl go free. That's safe enough. They've never seen any of us except when we've been wearing hoods. When we ferried them here, they were doped and out to the world. And Jimsy MacLean will make sure they keep their mouths shut afterwards."

"We only have to tell him that the police might be interested in finding that motor sailer," murmured Farrell, smiling coldly. "A dead man aboard would take some explaining—especially Mac-Phee, after the lobster raid. That's why we went to a lot of trouble putting him down there. Your brother's got problems enough already over Christie's death—except they can't pin anything on him firmly enough."

Fraser let out a long, whistling breath then jerked his head towards Carrick and Tara.

"What about these two?" he demanded.

"They're our problem." Farrell gestured the matter aside. "Small boat accidents happen—we can arrange a little story that will seem reasonable enough. What about it?"

Slowly, apparently reluctantly, Fraser nodded.

"How big a share?" he asked warily.

The question clinched it for Farrell and Peters, and they exchanged a grin.

"Enough for that new boat you want—plus." Strolling over, Peters prodded Carrick with a foot. "Up. We're moving the *San Helena* out of here, and you with it—insurance, in case anyone else gets curious. You too, Fraser."

"These ropes, then." Fraser gestured with his bound hands.

"They stay for now." Peters gestured reassuringly. "Purely temporary, but we'll fix that, and your shoulder, soon enough."

Muttering, Fraser struggled upright while Carrick did the same. But he wasn't finished.

"Do you people know the kind of risk in sailing out o' the Treshnishes after dark?" he demanded.

"Well enough," said Farrell dryly, freeing Tara from her chair then quickly retying her wrists. "Hell, it's a big enough nightmare in daylight—but that's our skipper's problem and Tessin says he can manage. Don't worry about your brother and the girl. We locked them up tonight with enough food and water to last a siege."

.   .   .   .   .

They left for the beach minutes later, the *San Helena's* men bringing the quickly bundled gear which had been in use at the old fort plus the two aqualung sets. Farrell detailed two of the

167

crewmen to paddle out with the packboat and the rest of the party squeezed aboard a folding dinghy which was lying at the water's edge.

The sea conditions hadn't changed. The same heavy swell was rolling in, chased by a fresh, occasionally gusting wind, and the two small craft tossed and heaved uncomfortably on the short trip out to the motor yacht.

All the time Carrick strained his senses against the night darkness and the noise of the sea, hoping for some sign or sight of Clapper Bell. He was certain the big Glasgow-Irishman was somewhere near and hardly idle—but all that happened was a sudden swirl in the water and the brief emergence of an inquisitive grey seal who followed them for a moment then disappeared again.

Once they were aboard the *San Helena* the dinghy was stowed and the packboat left tossing, secured by a line to the motor yacht's stern. Then, as the twin diesels began to purr and the crew prepared for sea, Farrell herded his three captives into the luxury of the big starboard cabin.

"Make yourselves comfortable," he said humourlessly, then shrugged at the expression on Carrick's face. "It's just one of those things, Carrick. I've never particularly wanted to kill anybody."

"It helps to know," said Carrick dryly. Fraser had flopped into an armchair, blood from his shoulder already staining the tasteful upholstery. "How about room service while we're here?"

"Maybe later," agreed Farrell acidly. He gestured with the automatic in his hand. "You and the girl—sit over beside Fraser. Nicely together."

They did as they were told and Farrell stood satisfied as Peters entered the stateroom accompanied by a crewman.

"Ready to go," said Peters shortly then pointed at Fraser. "We still got those fishing boats on the radar screen—about ten of them, a little west of here and still heading north. They're getting near. Is that normal?"

"Normal enough," muttered Fraser morosely. "They'll be heading round Ardnamurchan Point and prawning up there." He heaved himself upright a little. "Look, this shoulder of mine is giving me hell. You said—"

"We'll fix it, and soon." Peters chewed his lip for a moment, glanced at Farrell, then nodded. "Well, we won't worry about a few fishermen."

Farrell grinned a bleak agreement then handed his gun to the waiting crewman.

"Just watch them," he ordered. "All of them—and shoot if you've any trouble. Understand?"

The man nodded. Turning on his heel, Farrell left with Peters close behind. Left alone with his charges, the crewman dragged an armchair round to face them, dropped into it with a satisfied grunt, and held the automatic loosely on his lap.

In a few minutes they heard the rumble of the anchor being hoisted in then the *San Helena*'s diesels changed their note and the vessel began moving, pitching awkwardly as she turned then settling into a new, steady roll.

But her speed stayed low. The men on her cockpit bridge weren't taking any chances with the foul ground around them.

"Dan." Carrick leaned forward a little, ignoring the way their guard became instantly alert. "How much prawn fishing going on around Ardnamurchan these days?"

"Plenty," grunted Fraser. "Trawling mostly. There's money in it."

"Money." Carrick sighed and sat back. "That's always the answer." He glanced at Tara. "Know anything about fishing, Tara?"

She looked at him blankly, then shook her head.

"I've other worries," she said in a low, strained voice. "Like what's going to happen to us."

Carrick shrugged with a wry finality and fell silent, trying to gauge the *San Helena*'s progress. They'd swung to port as they left Sgeir Fionn and the diesels had only increased a few revolutions since. Probably they were out of the little sea-loch. Soon they'd be in a stretch of clear water, though there was still a heavy fringe of rock and reef on both sides.

Almost with the thought, the motor yacht's diesels quickened a little and glasses danced for a moment in their holders behind the little bar. The crewman in the armchair grinned and lit a cigarette.

And very, very gently, the stateroom door behind him opened and Clapper Bell slipped in, a noiseless, grim-faced figure whose black scuba suit glistened with wet.

Tara's eyes widened and her mouth opened a little. Then she quickly looked away.

A deck-plank creaked under Bell's feet, the sound almost lost under the vibration of the engines. But the crewman half-turned —then was jumping up, eyes widening, the gun in his hand swinging round, terror on his face.

The terror was still there as the bo'sun's diving knife sang across the stateroom and took the crewman deep in the throat. Still trying to claw towards it, the crewman died and crumpled on the carpeted deck.

"Didn't seem any sense in tryin' back on the island," said Clapper Bell apologetically. Bending over the crewman, he pulled the knife free and wiped it scrupulously on the carpeting. Then he came over and quickly cut the cords binding their wrists, talking as he worked. "I saw you were leavin', so I swam out an' tucked myself away 'tween decks for a spell." He glanced at Carrick. "But we'd better get the hell out o' this."

"Double quick." Carrick scooped up the automatic the crewman had dropped and gestured to Fraser. "Dan, you were lying about those fishing boats."

"Right." Fraser nodded hopefully. They both knew prawn trawling around Ardnamurchan Point didn't happen. For more reasons than the fact that any kind of trawling was illegal within three miles of the mainland. "It could be Jimsy MacLean organised something—"

"Or Shannon." Carrick helped Tara to her feet and grinned at her encouragingly. "Ready to go?"

"Where?" She stared at him, bewildered.

"Over the side." Carrick saw her eyes widen even more. "We'll cut the packboat loose and make for it. But jump as far clear as you can, and keep clear of those screws." He swung towards Bell. "How about outside?"

"Nobody near the stern," said Bell shortly. "They're all too damned worried about gettin' out of here. But I'll check."

He went out and came back in a moment, beckoning. They followed quickly and reached the empty stern. Travelling slowly under the cloud-filtered moonlight, the *San Helena* had already left Sgeir Fionn behind. Her faint wake hardly visible in the swell, white breakers showing where rocks began to port and a thinner, but equally dangerous line showing on the other side though further off, she was feeling her way down towards the open sea.

And the packboat was still tossing at her stern. Carrick reached the rail, found the packboat's painter line, then signalled to the others, the automatic held ready.

Fraser went over first, hitting the water cleanly and kicking out immediately, the peril waiting in the twin screws churning underwater cancelling the pain of his wounded arm. Clapper Bell and Tara followed, the bo'sun practically catapulting the girl out with him. As their heads surfaced Carrick let the packboat go, tucked the automatic carefully into his scuba suit's waterproof pocket, then glanced again towards the motor yacht's bridge. He could see the back of a man's head clearly. But the *San Helena*'s crew, as Bell had said, had other worries.

He jumped from the starboard rail and swam strongly for the drifting packboat. When he reached it, Clapper Bell already had Tara aboard and was dragging Fraser in.

Following Fraser into the heaving rubber hull, at least inches of water slopping around its floor, Carrick glanced back at the motor yacht.

She was almost a quarter of a mile away. But something was happening aboard her. He could pick out figures running on her deck, faint sounds which might have been shouts—and then he heard Clapper Bell curse. The *San Helena* was turning, her engines already quickening and the start of a bow wave gathering.

Squeezing past Tara, he reached the outboard motor at the same time as a spotlight came to life on the motor yacht's bridge and began wavering across the water. The first pull on the starter cord brought a splutter from the outboard, he tried again with a silent prayer, then gave a sigh of relief as it burst to life.

The spotlight caught them at the same moment. Bow on, the *San Helena* was thrashing down towards the packboat and closing the gap rapidly. Remembering the rifle, he shouted to the others to crouch down then rammed the outboard's throttle wide open. Responding with a full-throated bellow, the inflatable began moving as the first shot came from their pursuer.

Crouched down, Fraser, Bell and Tara lying prone on the rubber floor at his feet, he swung the tiller and sent the packboat skipping and bouncing to port. The spotlight wavered, caught them again, and another shot sang close to his head as he threw the packboat on a zigzag course.

But the *San Helena* was still gaining, her diesels thundering and that bow wave now a high, phosphorescent plume in the night.

"Clapper—" Carrick had to kick the bo'sun and shout again before Bell understood and crawled up beside him. Dragging the automatic from his pocket, Carrick handed it over then gestured at their pursuer "—try for the spotlight. I'll tell you when."

Bell nodded then grabbed for support as Carrick hurled the packboat into a tight, almost skidding turn which sent sheeted spray drenching over her length.

Suddenly they were heading back the way they'd come and almost parallel to the motor yacht, already inside the distance she'd need to make a following turn. Though she was trying, rudder hard over, deck rail awash as her power drove her on. Bell steadied himself again, waited for the peak of a swell, ignored two shots which whined overhead, and pressed the automatic's trigger.

The spotlight vanished. But the *San Helena* was still turning as before—and at the same moment the packboat's outboard coughed and lost its beat, coughed again, then stopped.

They were left as if dead on the water, while at thirty knots and fewer feet away the motor yacht rushed past them. Seconds later, the tumult of her wake hit the packboat side-on, throwing it bodily, clashing with the peak of a swell.

One moment Carrick was tugging hopelessly at the starter cord the next he was spluttering in the waves, thrown out beside the overturned hull. Tara surfaced beside him, then Clapper Bell appeared, swearing and gulping air, one large paw dragging Dan Fraser along until they could both grab the hull for support.

It was over now. When the *San Helena* came back—Carrick's thought ended there, drowned in a sudden cry from Tara.

"Over there, Webb—look."

"Look," urged Fraser at the same time in a hysterical whoop. "Look at them, Carrick! God, look at them!"

The *San Helena* wasn't coming back. She was slowing, turning away—and the reason was heading straight towards her, already not much more than half a mile distant.

Navigation lights twinkling to life one by one, a long line of fishing boats stretched the breadth of the clear water between the limiting breakers. Ten of them at least, they were coming on steadily, almost unhurriedly, but with a dogged, clearly defined purpose.

A rocket snarled skyward from the middle boat of the formation. It burst high over the *San Helena* in a searing white flare of light which hung in the sky, lighting the scene brighter than day. Then, as sharp eyes spotted something else on the fringe of the glare, another flare soared to burst above the overturned packboat and the figures clinging round it.

The flares lit something else, the regular, pattering splashes on the water beside each fishing boat, pattering splashes which reached out mysteriously to form an almost continuous line only to vanish moments before the lights guttered out.

"Nets!" Clapper Bell turned open-mouthed to Carrick in near disbelief and took a helping of sea water in the process. He spat it out, grinning now. "They've put down their flamin' nets. Let's see how those baskets get past that lot!"

And the fishing boats were still coming on. Treading water while the overturned packboat rose and fell in the swell, mere spectators temporarily ignored and forgotten, they watched the next stage in an awed, fascinated silence.

Any seaman knew what fishing nets could do to a small ship's propellers. Even large vessels had been completely disabled in that way—and on the *San Helena* at least one man had recognised the signs. The motor yacht idled under steering way for almost a minute while the little armada swept nearer, their formation exact.

Or almost exact. One boat near the extreme left was gradually dropping back, in apparent difficulties. In a few seconds there was a gap in the line—and the *San Helena*'s engines bellowed in a frantic search for full power as she punched forward.

Frantic light signals flashed along the line of fishing boats. A green rocket soared and burst from the middle boat in a final urgency as a shuffling attempt appeared to be made to close the gap.

Groaning to himself, Carrick saw it was all going to be too late. Speed still building, the *San Helena* was nearly there. He felt Tara grab his shoulder, then, even through the rubber of his suit, the tight grip of her nails. Clapper Bell was swearing again, he had an odd feeling that a noise like some strange, strangled laughter was coming from Fraser—and the motor yacht had reached the gap.

She foamed through, sending the nearest fishing boats tossing. Then suddenly, unbelievably, as if her rudder had been jammed over, she started to turn. But instead of turning the whole hull rose half out of the water, there was a scream of torn, mangled plating—and still driven on by that all-out power she was sinking. In a moment her bow had disappeared and her stern, the twin screws still spinning, was visible. In another moment, even they had vanished—and another white flare, bursting over the spot, showed only vast, gouting bubbles of air and debris.

And Fraser was still laughing in that same strangled, half-hysterical way. Laughing and slapping Clapper Bell repeatedly on the shoulder as if he would never stop.

"You knew," said Carrick hoarsely, understanding. "What's out there?"

"I knew—I hoped anyway." Fraser subsided from sheer exhaustion. "They'd have known too, if they hadn't panicked—it's on the charts. The Cailleach Rock, man—the Old Woman, we call her. Awash at low water, but always there. Like a big, sharp knife of solid granite. She must have cut the guts clean out of the murdering baskets."

He clung to the hull for another moment then grinned at them and gave a final chuckle.

"Man, I want to meet whoever dreamed up that notion. It was a bloody masterpiece—and if he was the devil himself I'd shake him by the hand."

. . . . .

Revelation came a few minutes later, when they were hauled aboard the lead fishing boat, a big drifter with a crew of soft-spoken East Coast men who had blankets ready to wrap round Tara and mugs of tea heavily laced with rum for all of them.

But there were Fishery Protection uniforms aboard as well— and Captain James Shannon stepped briskly from the wheel-house. He considered the scene gravely for a moment, then his round, bearded face twitched.

"You four are the most bedraggled quartet since Sinbad," he declared. A nod to the fishermen, and Tara and Fraser were hustled below to the warmth of the cabin while his smile broadened. "Mister, glad to see you in one piece. You too, bo'sun —and this time you didn't have all the excitement."

"We noticed," agreed Carrick politely.

"Well, the story can wait." Shannon rubbed his hands. "For the moment welcome aboard Her Majesty's Fishery Protection auxiliary—ah—" he paused and turned to the nearest East Coaster "—what's the name of this boat anyway?"

"The *Henrietta Appleyard O'Hagan*," said the East Coaster solemnly. "Our skipper named her after his ma."

"My God," said Shannon fervently, paling a little.

"Where's Jimsy MacLean, sir?" asked Carrick.

"Acting skipper of the *Razorbill*—out there." Shannon thumbed down the channel towards the rest of his pocket armada. "You can tell Fraser it was Jimsy who did that lame duck act. Between us, we had the whole operation sewn up."

Chuckling, he vanished back into the wheelhouse.

175

It was about an hour later before the fishing boats began to disperse. They'd recovered one live crewman, badly shocked, and a total of three bodies from the flotsam floating near the Cailleach Rock. Dirk Peters was one of the dead. But Farrell and the *San Helena's* skipper were among the missing who must be trapped somewhere below in the wreckage from the motor yacht's cataclysmic plunge.

And the finality of it all was still seeping through to the four from the packboat when Shannon came down to the *Henrietta Appleyard O'Hagan's* tiny fo'c'sle cabin with Jimsy MacLean beaming behind him.

"Happier now?" Shannon hesitated and clawed his beard with a slight embarrassment. "Well—you know what I mean, eh?"

"I'd say the word was 'grateful,'" Tara told him quietly. Her clothes had been dried at the galley stove, she'd borrowed a comb, and she looked almost herself again—but quieter, and with the red weal mark on her face as a reminder of the rest. Biting her lip, she glanced at MacLean. "Jimsy, I—well, I'm sorry for what I did. That's all I can say."

"Sorry?" Jimsy MacLean shook his head firmly, his black eyepatch gleaming in the cabin light. "From what I've heard, Farrell didn't give you much choice." He cleared his throat gruffly. "I know what pressure can be like so we won't talk about it. Understand, girl?"

She looked at him for a moment then nodded gratefully.

"Still, there are a few things to sort out," mused Shannon. "When Jimsy came storming into Port MacFarlane, bawling the odds and practically declaring a state of war on the Treshnish Isles, we didn't take too much time over details—"

"Like lobsters, you mean?" queried Dan Fraser wearily, easing his newly bandaged arm in its sling. "Look, Captain, as long as my brother—"

"We're heading for Sgeir Fionn now," said Shannon, cutting him short. "But lobsters? Yes, that's an interesting subject." His voice changed subtly, wry annoyance and grim amusement mixed equally. "With *Marlin* crippled, I went looking for other boats—and found the whole damned fishing fleet wanted to get involved. Why? Because someone had already spread the word that Dan Fraser had found the stolen lobster rafts—found them and said he wanted any reward money split among the raft owners who'd lost on the deal."

"Eh?" Startled, Dan Fraser stared at Jimsy MacLean and met a straight-faced nod.

"Personally, we may know another version." Shannon sucked his lips. "But we can't prove it. Agreed, Mr. Carrick?"

"It would be difficult," agreed Carrick solemnly.

"So between that and the bullet wound, you'll go back as a hero, Fraser." Shannon swallowed on the indignity. "But just as much as think of stepping out of line again and God help you. Is that plain enough?"

"Don't worry," said Fraser weakly. He drew a deep, relieved breath. "Well, that just leaves Roddy—"

"Roddy and Mhari," corrected Jimsy MacLean. "Better get used to her, Dan. She's likely to have her own way of keeping you two in order."

.   .   .   .   .

They landed at Sgeir Fionn ten minutes later and, led by Fraser, trekked by torchlight from the beach inland. The way was winding, climbing gradually, until they were halfway up the hill which dominated the island.

A tumbledown cottage appeared ahead, roofless and forlorn. Fraser slowed and gazed round almost apprehensively.

"Farrell said a cottage." He moistened his lips. "This is the only one I know on the island. A shepherd used to live in it."

"Then let's get them out, laddie," boomed Jimsy MacLean confidently, striding on.

The cottage was a hollow shell of four stone walls. But an innocent looking pile of debris in one corner of the stone flagged floor was just too neatly arranged to be true.

Carrick and Clapper Bell dragged it aside. Underneath was a trapdoor with a heavy padlock but half a dozen blows with a block of stone smashed it loose. Together, they eased the trapdoor back and Shannon shone a torch down into the black interior.

Two grimy but relieved faces looked up at them.

"What the hell took you so long?" demanded Roddy Fraser indignantly, an arm around his wife.

They got them out. Then Shannon beckoned Carrick and Bell aside, leaving the others and Tara in private conference for a spell.

At last, Jimsy MacLean left the little group and came over, shaking his head.

"I'm damned if I know," he said wearily. "James, that pair want to stay."

"Here?" Shannon blinked.

"Here," confirmed MacLean. "They want a tent, some stores and cigarettes—beyond that we've to get the hell out of it and come back in a week or so. They say they've a honeymoon to finish and it might as well be here."

For once, Shannon was left speechless.

"Why not?" Carrick considered the moonlit sea below and the way white breakers creamed in against the shore. "They could do worse."

MacLean sniffed, then fumbled in a pocket.

"Here," he said. "They want you to have this."

Carrick took the little scrap of red and gold wedding flag silk MacLean handed him, looked at it in the glow of the torchbeams, and knew it meant a great deal.

"Tell them I'll keep it for the silver wedding," he said quietly, then smiled at MacLean. "Well, your own problem is solved now, Jimsy. You've no need to sell Horsehead Island."

"True." Jimsy MacLean rubbed a slow, thoughtful hand along his chin. "Except Dan was telling me how much those oil folk might pay—"

"But damn it, you old goat," exploded Shannon. "I've a crippled ship, we've had death and disaster, there's a whole mess left to sort out—and all because you wouldn't sell!"

"An' what about all those ancestors you've got buried out there?" queried Clapper Bell, bewildered.

"There's that," admitted MacLean. Then he lowered his one good eye in a deliberate wink. "Mind you, if the price was right they could maybe be moved somewhere else. It could be done with a nice bit of reverence and ceremony. At the oil folk's expense, of course—"

"Dig them up," agreed Carrick mildly. "Why not?"

A long, rumbling growl began gathering in Shannon's throat.

Carrick tucked the scrap of wedding flag carefully into a pocket. Tara Grant was standing alone, he had things to talk about with her—and Shannon and MacLean looked set for a long, fiery session.